"Someone wants you dead!"

The Earl of Ware's hand grasped her elbow, preventing her from turning away. When he spoke again, his voice was gentle. "Emma, you can't hide from this."

Emma drew a deep, shuddering breath. "I appreciate your concern, my lord," she said mechanically. "But it is not your problem."

"Don't be a fool!" he snapped, his fingers tightening on her bare arm. "And don't be so damned polite! If you're trying to tell me to leave you alone, say so!"

"Very well. If you're now satisfied as to my well-being, why don't you leave?"

"Because I'm *not* satisfied," he said. "Emma, will you become my wife?"

THE IMPERILED
HEIRESS

JANICE KAY JOHNSON

Harlequin Books

TORONTO • NEW YORK • LONDON
AMSTERDAM • PARIS • SYDNEY • HAMBURG
STOCKHOLM • ATHENS • TOKYO • MILAN

Published September 1986
ISBN 0-373-31013-7

Printed in Canada

CHAPTER ONE

EMMA'S INHERITANCE from her godmother changed the fortunes—and expectations—of the rest of her family as well. Viscount Denton—Harry to his friends—fully expected his daughter to pay his gambling debts. Emma wasted no time in disabusing her father of that notion.

"I'm sorry, Papa, and I don't wish to seem niggardly, but it is not I who owe Squire Brume five hundred pounds. And this money is mine."

Emma felt she had earned every pound. Lady Brookings had had many admirable qualities, not least of which was her forthrightness and insistence on being honest to the point of bluntness, but those same qualities had made her a difficult woman to get along with.

For most of her life, Emma had spent several months a year with her godmother, and those had been trying times. Whenever Godmother was rude to Emma—and it was often—it had put her in a dilemma. If she "turned the other cheek," as her vicar believed a good Christian should, Godmother became even angrier and called Emma a "modern milk-and-water miss, good for nothing but needlework and bearing children," a subject Emma's mother most emphatically *never* discussed. But if Emma spoke her mind right back to Godmother, she got approval and a rousing fight, which, particularly as Lady Brook-ings aged, both tired Godmother and led to more honesty than was good for friendly relations. Thus, it was no wonder Emma felt she had earned her fortune.

Papa, of course, didn't understand her attitude in the least. "My dear," he said, in his most charming voice, as they sat together in his study, "we've always shared in this family. I don't think it's unreasonable for the rest of us to expect to receive some benefit from your good fortune. After all," he added, managing to look hunched, sad and fatherly (and most unnatural), "we are your only loved ones."

It was true Papa had always shared what little was left over after long nights at the gaming table, but Emma didn't feel the tiniest bit repentant.

"Of course I love you, Papa. And of course I'll help my family. I fully intend to give Georgiana a season in London with me, and naturally I'll pay for Charles to accompany us. However," she said, as she rose and started toward the door, "I know you won't want to leave the estate and I'm sure when you consider more deeply you'll find that receiving financial assistance from your daughter would be repugnant to you. Besides," she added, smiling sweetly around the door frame, "as you know, I don't approve of gambling!"

Papa would like nothing more than to accompany them to London and fritter away her fortune, but she had seen too much of the viscount's wastefulness. He would get nothing from her. Whatever Godmother's faults, she had managed to instill in Emma a strong-minded practical sense that had come in handy in the indigent past and, she could already see, would be even handier now that she had a fortune to protect.

Emma wasn't at all sure Lady Brookings would have approved of her using her money to help establish her sister and brother in society, but she did feel some sense of obligation and pity for them. Lady Brookings had detested Charles and Georgiana, both of whom she characterized as "brainless and weak." Emma thought the label a touch harsh. Weak they certainly were, but she believed that was owing to their upbringing, without the advantage of the escape once a year to Brook Hall and the bracing influence of Lady Brookings that Emma had experienced. Georgiana took after Mama: painfully shy, retiring, indecisive and impractical. And really, it was no wonder. Mama had been her only example. Charles was very much like Papa, but so far without his addiction to gambling.

Emma felt partly responsible for any weakness in her brother's and sister's characters. After Mama died, she had taken over, never really giving her younger siblings a chance to show their capabilities. She had felt she was the only one capable of managing the household accounts and the servants and making their small income suffice, but she wondered if she hadn't stifled Charles and Georgiana. If so, the least she could do now was give them a chance to establish themselves outside of the local sphere.

Emma's openhandedness was partly the result of a nagging sense of guilt, as well, because she had every intention of deserting her family after the London season. Part of her inheritance was Brook Hall. Emma's family, when they thought about the matter at all, assumed that she would sell the hall, but Emma fully intended to make it her home and she thought it might work out very well indeed.

It was a fine piece of property. The estate was well managed, the gardens were lovely without being elaborate, and the house itself dated from the Tudor period and was built of warm red brick and whitewashed timber. Emma had always loved the hall. It was perhaps not as handsome as the homes of some of the aristocracy, graceful Palladian designs constructed in marble and gray stone (Godmother called them "mausoleums"), but it was much homier. There were some very nice neighbors, and the property, unlike their Yorkshire home, was within an easy two days' journey of London with all its gaieties.

EMMA FOUND HER SISTER bent over her embroidery in the front drawing room, which, like the rest of the rooms, showed the effects of too few servants and too little money. After seating herself on the sofa next to the younger girl, Emma began without preamble. "Georgiana, I have just received a letter from Aunt Helen."

Her sister looked up from her tapestry. "Oh, what about? There's nothing wrong, is there? Is Uncle Max—?"

"In good health, so far as I know," Emma interrupted. "I wrote Aunt Helen asking her to sponsor us this season, and she's agreed."

Georgiana slowly set her needlework down. "Emma, how did you dare? She's never shown any inclination to help us before, and we hardly know her!"

"Not shown...? Georgiana, Aunt Helen has repeatedly offered to bring us out, but Papa has always refused. I thought you knew."

Her sister shook her head. "No, I had no idea. Papa never said..." She appeared lost in thought for a moment, then wailed, "But why? It would have been such a splendid opportunity for us! Especially for you! Why, you're almost too old now—" She broke off abruptly, blushing.

Emma smiled wryly. Probably her sister wasn't the only one who considered her, at twenty-one, on the shelf. Well, perhaps she was, but at least she wasn't desperate for a husband, now that she could afford an establishment of her own. And if she wanted a husband badly enough, she suspected she could find one, but she doubted that the silly young men, fresh from Oxford, who would undoubtedly be dancing attendance on her sister in between cockfights, curricle races and similar nonsense, would appeal to her anyway. If she were to fall in love, it would be with a man who possessed some principles and steadiness of purpose.

"Money," she said, in answer to her sister's question. "Although, of course, Uncle Max offered to pay the bills, Papa insisted he had too much pride to accept an offer of that sort, and he couldn't afford the expense himself."

"Oh." A soft sound escaped her sister's parted lips. "And now...?"

"We needn't rely on Papa."

Georgiana tucked her hand in Emma's. "It's very generous of you, Emma. You needn't do this for me, you know."

Emma smiled. "I want to, Georgiana. It will be a pleasure to watch you. With your looks you'll take the ton by storm."

And it was true enough, Emma thought, that if looks alone could create a sensation, Georgiana's would. She was a tiny girl with a mass of silvery-blond curls and bright blue eyes. With her rosebud mouth, finely molded features and porcelain skin, she was as exquisite as her needlework. Emma was positive droves of men would fall madly in love with her at first sight.

Now she smiled at her sister. "I can hardly wait for your first ball!"

"Ball?" Georgiana began to look vaguely alarmed. "You mean . . . a ball just for me . . . and you?"

"Yes, certainly. Aunt Helen wants to be sure to get a good date, so she said she would send a notice to the *Gazette* straight away."

"But . . . all those people will be *staring* at me! I thought we could just go to other people's parties! If we slipped in the door, no one would notice me especially and perhaps I could make a few friends. Emma," she said in a frightened voice, "I don't think I can do this. You know how I dislike meeting new people."

Emma had to hide her impatience. "Georgiana, it's every girl's dream! Wait until you tell Caroline about it. She'll be green with envy!"

Georgiana brightened at the agreeable prospect of telling her friend, but the pinched look about her mouth didn't disappear.

"And how can you find an eligible husband if you don't go to London?" Emma went on. "There's nobody locally who would even dare ask for your hand, much less be acceptable to Papa. Think what fun it will be in London to dance away the night with scores of handsome dukes and earls and . . . and possibly you'll even meet the Prince Regent! Aunt Helen moves in the very highest circles, you know."

Her reasonable tone didn't seem to be having the desired effect. "Think of the new gowns," Emma added enticingly. "Aunt Helen says she'll take us to her *modiste* first thing, since we don't want to appear provincial. She recommends that we study *La Belle Assemblée* to get an idea what styles we might want."

Georgiana glanced involuntarily at the magazine, which just happened to be lying near at hand. "There *was* a walking dress I particularly liked," she said. "It had tiny buttons down the front . . ."

"Then you shall have one just like it," her sister said encouragingly. "And, of course, Charles will be there to give his support."

"Oh! He didn't say anything!"

"Because I haven't told him yet. I wanted to speak to you first. Georgiana, Aunt Helen wants us to remove to London by next week at the latest. The first assembly at Almack's is less than a month away, and there's a great deal to do before then."

Georgiana gasped and fluttered. "But how can we? I can't be ready so soon! Perhaps in *two* weeks . . ."

"Why not?" Emma demanded in her most practical voice. "We have very little to pack. Most of our gowns won't be suitable for London. Papa will be staying here, so there's no need to worry about the house or the estate." Not that Georgiana ever did anyway. "We could quite easily climb into the carriage and depart in the morning, but there's no need to be that precipitate. I thought perhaps Thursday would do very well. Now," she asked, rising from the sofa, "do you know where Charles is?"

"Didn't he say something about taking a ride this afternoon?"

"Did he? Well, I'll speak to him later," Emma remarked as she left the room.

Although there wasn't a great deal for Georgiana to do before their departure, for Emma it was different. She wanted to be sure the servants were paid before she left, and she would visit all the tenants on the estate to find out what their needs were and what jobs had to be done so she could inform Papa before she left. Not that it would do much good, but it was certainly worth a try. A few roofs and fences might get mended, anyway, before the viscount's thoughts—and purse— moved on to other pastures. She set off to find Mrs. Hunt, the housekeeper.

Emma was so engrossed in her preparations that she was startled by the approach of the dinner hour. Fortunately, however, the maid had brought a pitcher of hot water to her room, so Emma had only to wash and to don the pale yellow muslin that had been laid out on the bed. She quickly brushed her hair and fastened it into a heavy knot, then gave herself a hasty scrutiny in the mirror. Such a severe hairstyle would never do in society, although she despaired of persuading her stubbornly thick, straight locks into the delicate curls currently in vogue. Her hair, the color of dark honey as it dripped from the pot, looked magnificent when it tumbled to her waist, but since she could scarcely thus appear in a ballroom, it seemed merely a liability. And she had allowed her skin to become lamentably dark, carelessness that would take time to remedy. She resolved to apply some Denmark lotion that night—Godmother had sworn by its efficacy. Her height, too, was bound to be a detriment, certainly to any man who sought a china doll to worship.

She made a wry face at herself in the mirror and turned away. Let them worship Georgiana! Godmother had always insisted that Emma's face, with its strong lines, slanting cheekbones and dark brows, had a good deal of character. Emma was well aware that character was not a quality admired by most men, but she could at least hope to meet one of the rare exceptions. In any case, she liked her looks well enough, and if they weren't what the ton currently admired, so be it. She would rather be able to take a high fence on her chestnut than have poems written to her "ethereal beauty."

Charles was late to supper, but since Papa, who would have been annoyed, had chosen to dine with Squire Brume, it scarcely mattered. Emma and Georgiana began without their brother, Emma listening with only half an ear to her sister's distressed monologue.

"I don't think I can do it, Emma," she repeated several times. "I just freeze when a stranger talks to me, and *everyone* in London will be strange! You know how I am. You've seen me at the assemblies." Resentment puckered Georgiana's pretty brow when she saw that her sister was listening with less than full concentration. "You just don't understand because nothing ever frightens you. You didn't inherit Mama's sensibilities, as I did!"

"I'm sure you're right," Emma agreed absently. Where was that foolish brother of hers? She prayed they wouldn't receive a message informing them that he had impulsively gone to a race meeting, or trout fishing in Scotland or something of the sort. Papa certainly wasn't plump in the pockets at the moment, so it was unlikely Charles was, but with him one never knew. Charles was given to odd fits and starts. He was no more cut out for the bucolic life than Papa, and it was a pity. Emma was certain the estate could be brought to pay better than it did at present, if only someone would lavish some time and money on it. Well, it was no longer her affair. Charles and Papa, between them, would probably let the land return to the wilds. And if Charles hadn't returned by Thursday, she and Georgiana would simply depart without him.

Her reflections were interrupted by Georgiana's peevish voice. "You haven't heard a word I said, have you?"

Emma blinked and returned her attention to her sister. "I'm afraid not," she apologized. "I'm sorry, Georgy. There's just so much to be done before Thursday, I fear I was letting my mind wander." Before she could begin to reassure her timid sister, however, the missing Charles appeared in the doorway, tugging at a wrinkled cravat. The haste with which he had changed for supper was all too evident.

"Sorry," he muttered, sliding into his place. "Horse threw a shoe."

"We started without you," Emma observed equably.

"So I see," he retorted. "I daresay it would have been too much trouble to have waited five minutes."

Emma watched as he dished up a mutton steak. "Since you didn't see fit to tell us your plans, we had no idea whether you intended to be home at all," she said.

"The damned food is cold," he grumbled, letting his fork drop with a clatter. "If we can't get a decent meal around here..."

Coldly, Emma interrupted. "The food was quite adequate when it was served. Don't blame Cook for your tardiness. And kindly watch your language."

She studied her brother's petulant face, wondering why they so often bickered. He was a handsome boy— no, at twenty-three, not a boy any longer. A man. He was unmistakably Georgiana's brother, with the same silver-blond curls that tumbled over a high brow, deep blue eyes and fine-boned features. Although he looked thin, no one could question his ability to master a fractious horse, or hold his own in a mill. The combination of an open, ingenuous face with a charming smile, when he chose to use it, had beguiled most of the neighbors into thinking him a delightful boy.

Emma did not feel as fond of her brother as she would have liked. It seemed to her that although he shared Georgiana's physical characteristics, he lacked her genuine sweetness of disposition. Emma, the closest to him in age, had never adored Charles as little girls were apt to do with an elder brother. Her childhood memories of him were either of being unkindly tormented or completely ignored. Perhaps if Charles had matured into a person she could have respected, it might have been different, but he hadn't. He cared little about learning to manage his inheritance, or his responsibilities toward his younger sisters.

Well, she couldn't blame him if he chafed at the restrictions of his life. The long cold winters in the north of Yorkshire could only be described as gloomy for one who wasn't able to occupy himself with the estate and had no bent for study. And even when the snows had melted, the hunting was indifferent. Charles, with no income of his own, was dependent on Papa for handouts. When Emma was home, she insisted on receiving the housekeeping money first, which no doubt increased her brother's resentment. Perhaps, she thought, cheering slightly, the proposed trip to London would improve their relationship.

Rather than withdrawing to allow Charles to enjoy his port in peace—or as he put it, "free from the tiresome chatting of females"—Emma said, "Charles, I'd like to speak to you."

"Something new to nag me with?" he inquired unpleasantly.

Emma drew a deep breath and silently asked the Lord for patience. "On the contrary. Aunt Helen has agreed to sponsor Georgiana and me this season. I don't need to tell you how much that means! We plan to leave for London Thursday morning. I'm hoping you'll accompany us."

"You want an escort, eh? Well, that wouldn't put me out," he conceded, and took a sip of the ruby wine. "I can spare a week. So Papa has finally agreed? Well, I'm glad. I daresay you'll do well, puss," he said generously, chucking Georgiana under the chin.

Since he had obviously not understood her invitation, and believed that they sought only his physical escort on the road, Emma was astonished at Charles's magnanimity. Surely he wouldn't be content to rusticate this spring while his sisters frolicked in the metropolis!

"You misunderstand," she said. "Georgiana would be grateful for your support during the season. Naturally, Aunt Helen assured me you would be entirely welcome at their town house, but if you should prefer to take lodgings, I'm sure they'll understand.''

"The season?" A frown darkened his brow. "It's all very well for you, but I can't afford it. There's no sense in going if a fellow can't take in the pleasures, and I hardly have the blunt for a new coat. It's all very well for you," he repeated in a tone of resentment.

"Naturally, I'll make you an allowance," Emma said calmly. "There is no reason Papa's gaming should condemn you to stay behind. Perhaps," she added, attempting to lighten the atmosphere, "we will all make advantageous marriages and our troubles will be at an end."

"*You* haven't got any troubles," he accused her, as though he wished she did. "Not but what it isn't generous of you, although I think you owe us that much."

"Owe?" Georgiana cried, surprisingly fired up in her sister's defense. "Emma doesn't owe us a thing! It's not as though Lady Brookings was any relation of ours. When I think of all Emma has done for us, and her generosity now, I wonder how you can be so ungrateful!"

Charles looked taken aback by the scorn on his sister's usually admiring countenance. "I'm not ungrateful," he protested. "But it's not as though Lady Brookings didn't know us all. I mean, she was a friend of Grandmother's. She could just as easily have been godmother to any of us!"

His expression clouded again as the injustice of it all swept over him, obviously not for the first time. Emma could just imagine the picture forming in his mind of himself as the heir, rather than her. Well, she wasn't going to waste any pity on him. If he chose to exert himself, he could turn the estate he *was* heir to into a profitable one, and it was his own loss if he refused to interest himself in drainage or new crops.

It was Georgiana who was Emma's first consideration. She had no doubt that Georgiana's dowry, as well as her own, of course, had been swallowed by Papa's imprudence. Georgiana's only hope was to make a respectable marriage, and with her beauty and the portion Emma intended to endow her with, she should do well, if only she, too, would exert herself. Unfortunately, Georgiana was perfectly capable of retiring into a frightened shell in the presence of strangers, and if she did that, then all Emma's efforts would be to no avail. Sometimes Emma was so consumed with impatience at her spineless sister and brother that she wondered at her ability to contain it, and found herself in complete sympathy with Godmother's disgust. This was one of those times.

"Charles." Briskly she interrupted her brother's self-pitying ruminations. "The justice of my being fortunate enough to be Lady Brookings's goddaughter is not relevant. The question is whether you desire to sojourn with us in London. You needn't put yourself out," she added dryly.

He drained the wine in his glass. "Well, if you really mean to give me an allowance . . ."

"Indeed I do," Emma said, wrinkling her nose at the strong, sweet smell of the wine. "Then that's settled. I think we should plan to leave as early as we can manage on Thursday. We're going to use the old coach; it would take too long to send for Lady Brookings's. I plan to take Lilac and Caspar for Georgiana and me to ride in town. John can ride one and lead the other, and he'll stay with us. Uncle Max says there's plenty of room in his stables, but I don't want to overburden his grooms. I expect you'll want to ride, instead of joining us in the coach?'' She raised one eyebrow and he nodded. ''You'll want to rent or buy a curricle and team in London, but we can worry about that later. Can you be ready to depart with no problems?''

"Naturally. I don't have anything to wear that's fit to be seen in London, and anyway my valet takes care of all that. Let's do get an early start; that coach is going to be slower than you remember,'' he warned. "I just hope Georgiana doesn't get motion sick.''

"Yes, indeed!'' Emma agreed fervently.

UNFORTUNATELY, Charles's prophecy proved correct; the coach was slower than Emma believed possible. The four heavy, plodding beasts that were all that Papa had available—he himself always rode one of his high-strung, expensive hunters—were able to move only slightly faster than Emma felt she could have walked, although Georgiana insisted that this was an exaggeration.

Each day Charles would swiftly lose patience and ride on ahead. Emma thought if she had to arrive one more evening at a posting-house, weary and aching in every bone, and find her brother comfortably ensconced in the coffee room, tankard in hand, chatting with the locals and looking despicably refreshed and comfortable, she would throttle him.

Georgiana did in fact become travel sick. Most of the time the coach moved too slowly for that to happen, but on the rare occasions when the horses were able to work up a brisk clip, usually downhill, Georgiana's face would become tinged with green and she would huddle in the corner clutching at her stomach.

These recurring bouts of nausea, along with her
steadily growing fear of the prospect in store for her,
made Georgiana miserable company. Emma tried to
entertain her sister by reading aloud from a guide-
book to the various counties they were passing
through, but Georgiana failed to display the slightest
interest in ruined abbeys or any other points of local
interest.

The various posting-houses and inns where they
broke their journey were reasonably comfortable, but
living out of boxes soon palled. Emma could never
recall finding a journey so tedious, but she concluded
that it was because Godmother's horses and carriage
had compressed the miles into a much shorter space of
time on her previous trips. By the end of the first day,
she deeply regretted her decision not to send for what
was, after all, her own carriage.

On the last day Charles had, as usual, preceded
them, and no sooner had the coach pulled up at their
aunt's house in Berkeley Square than a footman flung
open the door of the handsome gray mansion and
Aunt Helen came hurrying down the steps to meet her
nieces.

Aunt Helen was Papa's sister, and in part she shared
his cheerful, haphazard outlook on life. She, however, had a good deal more sensitivity and a kinder
heart, and her lack of practicality was easily offset by
her husband, who was shrewd indeed. Helen Barlow
was a plump woman whose bright, unlined face be-
lied her years.

Her round face was beaming now in genuine delight at seeing her nieces, and Emma tumbled from the
coach to hug her aunt.

"Aunt Helen, it's wonderful to see you! And wonderful of you to invite us!"

"Oh, pooh!" the older woman disclaimed. "This will be the most exciting season in years! I just wish we could have done it long ago! But I shouldn't rattle on. You girls must be exhausted." As Georgiana climbed wearily down the steps, Aunt Helen turned to her. "And Georgiana! You poor dear!" She drew the pale, trembling girl into a comforting embrace. "Come into the house this instant. A hot bath and a warm glass of milk will be just the thing, and I'm sure you must be longing to lie down."

She ushered the girls up the steps and into the entrance hall, a footman following close behind with the first of their luggage. Even Emma wasn't averse to the program outlined by her kindly aunt, and within half an hour found herself tucked under a warm quilt, her eyelids growing heavy. Tomorrow would be time enough to let herself become excited about the weeks to come.

CHAPTER TWO

THE NEXT FEW DAYS went far better than Emma had dared hope. The one aspect of the coming season to which Georgiana had genuinely looked forward was the acquisition of a new wardrobe, and the morning after their arrival Aunt Helen arose at what Emma was sure was an unwontedly early hour and, upon being assured that both girls felt sufficiently rested, urged them out of the house and into the waiting carriage.

Her modiste, Madame Lisette, situated in Bruton Street, was clearly delighted to have charge of the outfitting of two attractive young ladies of apparently unlimited means. This was one part of the season Emma was not prepared to stint on. Georgiana's beauty was certainly her best asset in the husband-hunting game, and Emma wanted to ensure that her beauty was suitably framed. As for herself, she wasn't averse to a little admiration if Madame Lisette could help her garner some, and, anyway, she was very fond of pretty clothes.

Georgiana was easy to dress, as her china-doll looks and pale coloring exactly suited the accepted mode for young ladies in their first season. Her gown for Aunt Helen's ball was to have an overdress of silver lace, touched with spangles, worn over white satin. Muslin morning dresses of palest pink and a delicate shade of lilac, a walking dress in cerulean blue, with a border of cable trim in a darker blue, and a satin pelisse in a deep blue trimmed with mink were promptly decided on.

Emma had to argue strenuously with her aunt, aided by Madame Lisette, to keep from being dressed in the same youthful pastels. Her honey-colored hair, gray-green eyes and tanned cheeks needed a more dramatic backdrop, and Aunt Helen's objections soon faded when she saw how handsome her niece looked in the right gown.

Emma chose an evening gown in amber Italian taffeta, another in sea-green crepe worn over a paler slip of sarcenet, and yet another in marigold Berlin silk, as well as many walking and morning dresses, a riding dress in Hessian blue, a fawn-colored silk pelisse trimmed with braid and another in sage-green velvet edged with chinchilla. Emma was almost amused to observe her aunt's surprise. It had been brave of Aunt Helen to offer to take on a niece who she clearly had anticipated would present a dowdy appearance.

Madame Lisette appeared more interested in the challenge of turning Emma out to her best advantage than in the simple task of adorning Georgiana's beauty. Perhaps she felt Emma would be more of an advertisement to her skill than Georgiana, who, after all, would have looked lovely in sackcloth.

Their cousin Alex, a tall, cheerful young man active in his father's business, volunteered to introduce Charles to town life, and Emma was relieved that they seemed to take to each other. She overheard them talking eagerly, and somewhat boyishly, about cockfighting in Clerkenwell, Alex also extolling the fun of bearbaiting. Emma thought both activities sounded disgusting, and shouldn't be allowed, but she had resolved to leave Charles on his own, so long as he did his part with Georgiana and didn't run over the allowance she was prepared to make him.

She had provided Charles with funds immediately, and Alex soon bustled him off to his tailor, Herr Schultz, who apparently cut garments in the military fashion, much to the taste of his young clientele, as well as to Baxter's for hats and Hoby's for boots. Alex was able to help Charles find lodging at a good address in Bennett Street—he evidently lived nearby—and Charles moved out, although he left his horses in Uncle Max's stables.

As SOON AS the girls' gowns arrived, they began the series of morning calls that Aunt Helen insisted were essential to a successful season. One of their first visits was to an old friend of hers, Lady Hartley, whose daughter, Julia, was Georgiana's age and also prepared to make her come-out. This damsel was a complete contrast to Georgiana, having dark hair and eyes and rosy lips and cheeks, as well as a vivacity of manner that was foreign to Georgiana.

The moment the sisters entered the Hartley drawing room in Aunt Helen's wake, Julia hurried forward to take Georgiana's hand. "We'll be absolutely splendid together!" she cried. "Mama, look! Night and day! Oh, do say you'll go driving with us tomorrow."

Georgiana blushed and lowered her eyes, and mumbled something unintelligible. Emma couldn't entirely blame her, as she thought the girl rather overwhelming, as well as being somewhat immodest, but Julia's mama merely smiled fondly and said, "Of course she must come with us. I hope you girls will become best friends."

Julia didn't appear to notice Georgiana's lack of response and led her to a sofa, chattering all the while. Lady Hartley smiled apologetically at her other guests and said, "Don't mind Julia! She's very high-spirited, but doesn't mean any harm. I'm sure your niece's charming modesty will serve as a good example to her! Do sit down," she added, gesturing to another sofa. "Mercifully, Lady Cowper is a dear friend of mine, because I would hate to have had to present Julia to Mrs. Drummond-Burrell in the expectation of receiving vouchers. She doesn't care at all for young ladies with minds of their own! Do you have vouchers yet?"

Mrs. Barlow shook her head. The treasured vouchers to Almack's were the object of the campaign she had been planning since she had first invited her nieces for the season, because although she herself was well acquainted with most of the patronesses, and therefore reasonably confident of receiving the vouchers, one never knew when they would take a girl in dislike and exclude her. This was social disaster, and she was determined that her nieces should be accepted everywhere.

"No," she said, "we've just barely made the girls presentable. I believe we'll call on Lady Cowper on Wednesday."

On the short drive home to Berkeley Square, Emma asked her sister how she and Julia had gotten along. "She seemed...perhaps a little forward to me," she commented.

"Oh, no!" Georgiana protested vehemently. "I thought her delightful! She has such a kind heart. I only wish I could talk half as interestingly, and with such . . . such spirit. Don't you think her a lovely girl, Aunt Helen?''

Aunt Helen, once appealed to, agreed that indeed she did, and she and Emma exchanged pleased, and conspiratorial, smiles. In Julia's company at a ball, it would be impossible for Georgiana to hide in the corner. Emma had no doubt Julia would ruthlessly drag her new friend in her wake, and it would be all to Georgiana's good.

Emma, too, had been included in Lady Hartley's invitation to drive in Hyde Park at the fashionable hour of five o'clock the following day, but Uncle Max had earlier asked if she would care to ride with him, and she decided to accept his invitation. Caspar had been woefully neglected while Emma pursued her new wardrobe, and she was eager to shake the fidgets out of the big chestnut. Also, her blue riding dress had been one of the first delivered, and in it, with the matching low-crowned hat topped with a curling ostrich feather perched rakishly on her head, Emma was conscious of looking her very best.

She had long since decided that Uncle Max was her favorite relative. Godmother had told her that Max Barlow had not been thought a very good match for the Viscount Denton's daughter, being the possessor of no more than a respectable fortune, but Helen had been deeply in love, and, after all, there was nothing objectionable, so the family allowed the marriage.

Uncle Max, however, had proved to have a good head for finance, and in the intervening years his fortune had multiplied many times over. He had done well on the Exchange, he was known to have an interest in trade with the East (this activity was tacitly ignored by even the stuffiest members of the ton), and his half-dozen estates were farmed with the newest methods and turned a reasonable profit.

Emma was confident of her uncle's assistance, should either Georgiana or Charles prove to be a problem. Indeed, he had already given her invaluable advice on how to handle her new fortune, and she had taken her affairs to his man of business, Mr. Clampett.

Uncle Max had warned her that the ride in the park would not be what she was accustomed to, and that they were unlikely to achieve more than a slow canter, but she was still amazed by the size of the crowds walking, riding and driving. Traffic was constantly clogged as horsemen paused to chat with gaily dressed ladies in carriages, who peeped flirtatiously up from under ruffled parasols, or as gentlemen in curricles stopped to take friends up. Emma hadn't quite realized what a social gathering this was, for the sole purpose of enabling people to see and be seen.

She would have been sorrier to lose her anticipated gallop, except that she was conscious of a number of admiring glances turned her way, and several young gentlemen pressed Uncle Max for introductions. By the time they reached the end of the loop and turned back, Emma had collected a small cluster of admirers, all of whom kept a safe distance because Caspar was not entirely sure he cared for this ride. Emma had no doubt of her ability to control the rangy animal, but his occasional flailing hooves and snapping teeth were disconcerting to the other horses. In future, she hoped she could exercise him at another time of day.

They had just stopped to exchange remarks with Lady Hartley and the two girls in their barouche when Emma's eyes were drawn to an approaching horseman. Initially it was the horse that caught her attention, not the rider. He was a magnificent charcoal-gray stallion, more powerfully built than most. As they drew closer, Emma could see the bunched muscles and wicked eye. This definitely wasn't an ordinary mount.

Nor was the rider ordinary. Even though he was astride, it was possible to tell that he was an unusually big man, broad of shoulders and chest. He had an angular face, almost gaunt, that couldn't be described as handsome, although it was certainly compelling. His dark hair was brushed into the windswept style, and his shoulders were covered with a slate-blue coat that fit like a glove. His eyes, a dark, stormy blue, met Emma's, and she blushed to realize she had been staring.

"Richard!" Uncle Max cried, also spotting the newcomer. "Good to see you. Have you been out of town? Come meet my nieces."

The man politely steered his horse over to the barouche, and he exchanged a pleasant greeting with Lady Hartley, who actually appeared mildly flustered by his presence.

"Girls," she said, "this is the Earl of Ware. Ware, I'd like you to meet my daughter, Julia, and—" she nodded at Georgiana, who was shriveling away from his stare "—Georgiana and Emma Denton."

The party of riders soon took their leave of Lady Hartley and her charges, and proceeded on. Emma was surprised that the earl stayed with their group, and in fact soon reined his horse in to ride next to her.

Unfortunately, his mount and Caspar took each other in instant dislike, although the earl's horse was too well disciplined to act on his feelings. Caspar, however, screamed a shrill challenge and reared, pawing the air with his hooves. Emma sawed at the reins and soon got all four feet back on the ground, but by this time she was the cynosure of all eyes, and flushed with embarrassment and annoyance.

Lord Ware sat his horse, unmoving, and laughed. "Really," he mocked, as they once again progressed forward, Caspar sidling and twisting, "you should school that animal."

Emma had been staring straight ahead, her jaw clamped firmly shut. Now she turned to him, her eyes blazing, and said, "If you would remove that vicious beast you're riding, we'd be fine!"

"Vicious beast?" His face took on a look of hurt surprise. "How can you say that? His behavior is impeccable."

And of course it was, although the stallion's eyes were rolling wildly, showing the whites. Emma turned her smoldering gaze back to the hindquarters of Uncle Max's bay, well in front of her. She couldn't even pretend to carry on pleasant conversation with someone else while she regained her composure, since the other riders had scattered when Caspar began acting up.

She wasn't entirely sure why she was so angry with the earl, or why her emotions were churning. She had been very rude to him, with no cause, and she certainly owed him an apology. Nevertheless, she had to take several deep breaths and talk very sternly to herself before she could turn her head, with a semblance of her normal expression on her face, and say, "My lord, I'm sorry I snapped at you. I fear you are entirely right about Caspar. I've never had any difficulty with him before, but he doesn't appear suited to this kind of traffic."

"Your first day?"

She nodded.

He shrugged, then, to her surprise, said, "Oh, he'll settle down. What you need to do is give him a good run."

"I thought this would be exercise for him," Emma admitted ruefully. "I'm afraid I didn't quite picture such a throng." She gestured vaguely at the milling crowd.

"Best time to come out is in the morning," he said. "Will you join me tomorrow? Has to be early...say, seven?"

Emma wondered why her pulse had speeded up, and her hands felt unsteady on the reins. "I'd be delighted," she said. "I hope," she added, casting a doubtful look at her horse, who chose that particular moment to snort and toss his head wildly, "Caspar behaves."

"Oh, Thor here wouldn't dare get in a fight, if that's what you're worried about. We could have a race, though." He grinned, and his eyes held a distinct challenge.

"Certainly," she said, her chin rising.

"Why haven't I seen you in town before?" he asked abruptly.

"I'm flattered that you think you would remember me," she responded demurely. She wondered in sudden horror if she was trying to flirt with this man. Surely that would be a mistake.

"I'm good friends with your uncle. I'd know if he had a niece out."

"Oh," she said, feeling dampened, then explained, "This is my first season."

Those strange blue eyes were studying her intently, as though he were puzzled by something. However, Uncle Max, unnoticed by Emma or Lord Ware, had allowed his horse to drop back and was suddenly at Emma's side.

"Shall we go home, Emma?" he asked cheerfully. "Or do you care to take another turn?"

She shuddered. "I think not. Heaven only knows what Caspar would do. I'd hate to gain a reputation as the woman with the wild horse before I've even met anybody."

Ware was smiling. "Don't I count as somebody?"

She blushed and stammered, "Oh, I meant…" Why did he make her feel so gauche?

"And I thought I was too large to overlook! Well, I'll see you at the club, Max. Miss Denton, seven o'clock?"

"Yes, indeed," she agreed, still trying to regain her composure.

He flicked a casual hand at them and was soon clattering away at a speed that seemed precipitate for the busy London streets. Emma was only aware she was staring after him when she heard Uncle Max say "Emma?" in a voice that indicated it wasn't the first time he had tried to capture her attention.

She felt her cheeks reddening again and cursed the effect the earl appeared to have on her. She hadn't blushed in years, and here in the space of one hour she seemed to be turning into the sort of simpering miss at whom Lady Brookings would have sneered.

"I'm sorry, Uncle Max. My mind was wandering. Shall we go?"

AT THE SUPPER TABLE that evening, Aunt Helen succeeded in worming an account of the afternoon from her nieces. Emma found herself describing every gentleman she had conversed with, what he had said, and what her reaction to him had been. For each, the older woman would tack on a gentle comment of warning.

Although for some unaccountable reason Emma was reluctant to talk about the earl, to avoid any appearance of partiality she felt constrained to mention that she had ridden with him. Her aunt brightened immediately.

"Ware? How delightful! I had no idea he was in town. I hope you found him agreeable? I know his manner sometimes seems abrupt, but with those looks..." She shivered delicately. "I understand he has at least twenty thousand a year, not to mention the title. If one of you girls could attach *him*...! But of course that's foolish. Don't get your hopes up. He's been the most sought-after bachelor in England for I don't know how many years, and he absolutely ignores women!"

Her husband cleared his throat.

She cast an irritated look his way. "Well, of course not *that* kind of woman, but he's never been known to have even a *flirtation* with an eligible young lady. It's terribly exasperating to all the mothers! Personally, I always found it amusing, although now I can see..." A frown creased her usually placid brow. Just as Emma opened her mouth to disclaim any marital designs on the earl, Aunt Helen hurried on with fresh enthusiasm. "Well, what did he say to you? Or was he merely polite?"

"I'm not sure I would describe him as polite at all," Emma said with a chuckle. "Although I must confess that was partly my fault. Caspar was positively horrid; he didn't care for the traffic at all, you see, so he put on quite a show. But in the end Lord Ware was really very nice. In fact . . ." She hesitated, then reluctantly went on, "I'm riding with him in the park tomorrow morning. Just to exercise Caspar, you know. I gather the earl rides most mornings. It was kind of him to invite me."

During this speech Aunt Helen straightened in her chair and her face glowed. "Well!" she exclaimed, visibly gratified. "He invited you . . .! Just fancy that!"

Mr. Barlow interrupted her rhapsodies. "I think it would be best not to read too much into one invitation, don't you, dear? After all, he is a friend of mine, and he may have felt that common politeness required him to make some show of interest."

Aunt Helen's bosom, which had been swelling with the anticipation of sweet victory, collapsed, and Emma herself felt a distinct lowering of spirits.

She hastened to agree with her uncle, however. "Indeed, I'm sure you're right, Uncle Max. I'm certain his kindness was no more than one might expect to the niece of a good friend."

"It might be," Aunt Helen conceded reluctantly. "But still . . . he must be getting to the age where he feels a need for the comfort of a wife and heir. Perhaps—"

Her husband interrupted once more. "He has no fewer than five nephews, of whom I believe he is very fond."

"Oh, pooh!" Aunt Helen looked very much as though she would have liked to stick her tongue out at her husband, but good manners restrained her, so she turned to Georgiana instead.

"Well, my dear, whom did you meet today? I'm certain Lady Hartley must have introduced you to the notice of some gentlemen."

It appeared that she had, and Georgiana rather shyly listed an imposing number of names and titles. In response to Aunt Helen's inquiry whether any had impressed her, a delicate blush mantled Georgiana's cheeks. "There was a gentleman who was particularly kind to me," she said softly. "His name is Sir James Finkirk. He was very handsome."

"A gazetted fortune hunter!" Aunt Helen said with a frown. "I'm surprised Lady Hartley allowed you to speak to him."

"She seemed a little annoyed," Georgiana admitted. "There was *such* a crowd around the carriage, though. She never said what she didn't care for. And surely he has much too...too noble a face to have such motives!"

Emma interjected, "And, of course, Georgiana doesn't have a fortune."

"Yes, that's true," Aunt Helen agreed. "We must just make sure he realizes that. There is bound to be some confusion, you know, when one of you is known to be wealthy. Many people may assume the other is, also. Max..." She turned to her husband.

He nodded. "I'll find some discreet way of spreading the word in the clubs. Someone is certain to ask me, anyway. We don't want Finkirk's kind hanging around."

Aunt Helen touched Georgiana's hand. "I'm sorry, my dear. Even if he isn't interested in you for your money, I'm afraid he's dreadfully unsuitable. Not two guineas to rub together, and always just ahead of the duns. I'm really surprised to hear he's back in town this year. I can't imagine too many tradesmen will be giving him credit."

The subject was allowed to drop, although Emma observed a mulish set around her sister's mouth that rather surprised her. Georgiana was generally the most biddable person imaginable, and it certainly wouldn't be like her to defy what amounted to an order. It didn't sound as though Finkirk would be welcome at the more exclusive entertainments, anyway, so most likely they had heard the last of the man.

Emma was determined to treat the earl with friendly reserve, appropriate to her uncle's friend. She most emphatically wouldn't want him to think that she had, no matter how temporarily, imagined seeing a spark of interest in his eyes. She scolded herself for being so foolish as to allow the first handsome man she had met in London flutter her heart for even a moment.

AT PRECISELY SEVEN O'CLOCK in the morning Emma allowed the groom to boost her up, and was just settling in the saddle, collecting the reins and catching her breath, when she heard the clatter of hooves that presaged the earl's arrival. When he offered her a bow and a dazzling smile that lent his face a wicked charm, her resolve of the night before suffered a setback. Her pulse definitely speeded up, and she felt it was a credit to her self-control that she managed to nod her head and smile coolly in return.

"My lord."

"Miss Denton." He mimicked her manner. "Shall we go before that brute you're riding paws a hole in the ground?"

"That *was* the object this morning, wasn't it?" To her fury, she saw that his own stallion, although giving every evidence of being even more tightly wound than yesterday, was still under perfect control. Emma had always considered herself a good horsewoman, but her pride was wilting in the face of this master.

Both were kept fully occupied in maneuvering their restive mounts through the early-morning traffic of wagons loaded with produce and outbound coaches. It was a relief to turn in the gates of the park and find the dusty path and greensward empty but for a few other horsemen.

Lord Ware raised one eyebrow. "Like a head start?"

"Certainly not!" Emma snapped. "Are you ready?"

At the earl's grin, both loosened their reins and dug their heels into the animals' sleek sides. Emma was momentarily surprised by the explosion of energy under her, but the flash of panic gave way to exhilaration. She leaned low over Caspar's neck and felt the wind whip her hair from its knot and tangle strands across her face. Her watering eyes nearly blinded her, but she could see the surging muscles of the gray drawing away.

Thor won, of course, but Emma couldn't be especially sorry. The pleasure had been in the run itself, and the wild freedom, not in the competition. When she pulled Caspar up she saw that the earl, too, was laughing, and she thought for a moment how different he was from her image of the London beau. Unfortunately, that thought brought others on its heels, and she remembered that she was in London, not the wilds of Yorkshire, and that she must look a fright.

With a gasp she fumbled with one hand for the pins hanging loose in her tangled hair, which had fallen down her back. She had a vision of that moment in front of her mirror when she had tried to imagine entering a London ballroom with her hair hanging to her waist. Well, this wasn't quite that bad, but bad enough. She sneaked a quick glance at the earl and found his dark blue gaze caressing her with a half-amused look that sent a flash of exhilaration through her, until she felt almost as excited as she had during the reckless race. Then annoyance replaced that inexplicable thrill. With a characteristic and, she had been told, unfeminine militancy, her chin rose and she said coldly, "You needn't laugh. If you were a gentleman, you would look the other way!"

The glint of laughter in his eyes mocked his serious tone. "Ah, but surely by this time you've been told that I have a *most* ungentlemanly reputation!"

"You flatter yourself," she retorted sharply. "People *do* have something else to talk about, you know. And it's rather childish to brag about a bad reputation, don't you think?"

"No doubt you're right." He was still smiling. "However, this time I *will* be a gentleman and suggest we walk our horses in the shrubbery while you repair your coiffure...although I greatly prefer your hair as it is now."

Emma sent a smoldering look his way, but really she had no choice, so she waited while he dismounted, then accepted his hand as she slid off Caspar. He took the reins of both animals as they turned into one of the small paths that led between flowering shrubs.

Emma ran her fingers through her tangled locks, then twisted her heavy hair up and stuck the pins back in. How she wished she had worn a hat to cover the worst of her dishevelment!

Lord Ware's voice at last broke the silence. "Shall we turn back? You look respectable enough to me now."

"I doubt that," she said dryly, "but I've done my best. And, yes, do let's turn back."

The earl was a very big man. Emma was accustomed to looking most men straight in the eyes, but the top of her head barely came up to his shoulder. This was the first time she had seen him off his horse, and his own physical impact was even greater. The fashionable skin-tight garments were flattering to him as they were to few men, and although he was powerfully muscled, she noticed he moved with a casual grace that was disconcerting.

Emma made herself smile brightly up at him and say, in a chatty tone, "I'm sure I'll be in disgrace with Aunt Helen when I arrive home looking such a ragamuffin, but the run was worth it! Even Caspar looks the better for it."

The chestnut was ambling along next to Thor, looking as placid as a cart pony. Emma reflected wryly that he would probably act up again as soon as she was back in control; he probably recognized that it would be foolish to start a quarrel with the man who now held the reins.

"Would you care for a rematch someday?"

"I'm afraid it wouldn't do me any good. Although," she said with dignity, "Caspar is laboring under a disadvantage."

"Oh?" He gave her a sidelong look, that same amusement in his eyes.

"The sidesaddle. Think how difficult to run it would be with the weight on your back so ill-distributed. Now if I were able to ride astride..."

"You would never gain entrance to Almack's," he said quellingly. Just as she was certain she had been too bold, and that he had taken her in disgust, he added thoughtfully, "However, you have a point. We certainly must have that rematch."

Emma turned to regard him in astonishment.

He saw her stare and laughed. "Don't be foolish! Not here, of course! Maybe at Stanwood. Devilish uncomfortable place, but nobody sees anything he isn't supposed to. We could find some breeches for you."

Emma was speechless. Just what was he suggesting? She had heard of his main seat, Stanwood Castle. Because of its historical interest, it had been mentioned in the guidebooks she had read on the road south; evidently the central keep dated from the Norman period. Historical interest apart, however, she was hardly likely to be visiting the bachelor Earl of Ware at his country estate in the near future!

The man seemed to have an uncanny ability to read her thoughts, because his mouth turned up in that mocking half smile and he remarked, "I wasn't suggesting an elopement. No need to look so panicked. I do have house parties occasionally, and I thought you might accompany your uncle sometime, that's all."

Emma felt foolish. What's more, it was annoying that he seemed to find so much in her to amuse him; she was beginning to feel like a comedy act.

Tartly she said, "An elopement is the last thing I imagined you were suggesting! Now, if you would help me mount...?"

With his infuriating laugh ringing in her ears, she turned her back and waited for a leg up, which he obligingly gave. Determined to hide her own discomfiture, she waited until he had mounted, then turned Caspar back the way they had come. Calmly she said, "Perhaps you would tell me who some of the other riders are, if I'm likely to see them about town. I've met scarcely anyone as yet."

"Oh, you'll meet them soon enough. Too soon, with most of them. Shall we canter instead?" Without waiting for a response, he loosened the reins and allowed Thor to quicken his pace.

Caspar eagerly followed suit. Emma was exasperated at having her conversational gambit so indifferently dismissed, but if pressed she would have had to admit to a certain relief. And, after all, exercise was what they had come out for, wasn't it?

They took several nearly silent turns up and down the loop, until the horses had broken into a gentle sweat. The return trip to Berkeley Square was far more sedate than the outward-bound journey had been, with both horses pacing quietly, Caspar as well mannered as Emma could have desired. When they arrived at the stables, the groom held the reins while Emma dismounted.

She tilted her head back and offered the earl, who had made no move to dismount, a pleasant smile, saying, "Despite appearances, I *did* enjoy our ride. Thank you for the suggestion."

"We must do it again soon. Although..." The wicked light was back in his blue eyes. "Perhaps we should wait until you are well established in society. If Mrs. Drummond-Burrell could see you now..."

Emma had almost been back in charity with the man. Now she glared up at that dark face and snapped, "Why Uncle Max is so fond of you I'll never understand! Now if you'll excuse me..." She turned away and, back stiff and head held high, walked up the stairs, skirt in one hand, and into the house. The back of her neck prickled from her awareness that he must be watching. The man had no idea of courtesy!

Almost immediately she encountered Georgiana in the upper hall. Her sister's rosebud mouth dropped unbecomingly open. "Emma! What happened to you? Did you have a fall? Are you all right?"

Emma was not in her best frame of mind. "I certainly didn't have a fall," she responded frigidly. "It was simply windy. *If* you'll let me pass, I could do something about my appearance before Aunt Helen sees me."

Her sister blushed and moved aside, letting Emma sweep by and down the hall. Once she was safe in the bedchamber, her gaze instantly found her reflection in the mirror, and she stared in horror. She looked like a wild Gypsy, her hair a tangled mop, with loose tendrils about her face and a few pins sticking out, her face flushed (just from the wind, she told herself) and her eyes sparkling dangerously. She felt like crying.

Finally she tugged on the bellrope and began yanking pins from her hair as she waited for the maid. There was no sense in repining. Undoubtedly she had made a fool of herself, but she wasn't likely to encounter the Earl of Ware often, and in any case, it didn't matter what he thought of her. As Uncle Max's friend, he would surely be polite (as polite as he was capable of being), and in the future she would try to behave like the poised adult she was, and that was the

end of the matter. Now she had best whip herself in
shape, for today was the all-important call on Lady
Cowper.

CHAPTER THREE

SEVERAL HOURS LATER, Emma ruefully surveyed her
reflection in the gilt-edged mirror. Mabel, Aunt Hel-
en's very capable dresser, had employed her best efforts on Emma's behalf, but the end result was less
than satisfactory. Her cheeks were still unbecomingly
flushed, and while the tangles had been brushed out,
her always unruly hair had been rendered totally un-
manageable by the wind. The heavy locks were pinned
on top of her head in the current Grecian mode, but
tiny tendrils persisted in escaping to wave wildly about
her face. The modest muslin gown, selected to meet
Aunt Helen's notion of what Lady Cowper would
consider suitable for a young lady in her first season,
was too demure to flatter Emma's more dashing style.
Altogether, she reflected, it would scarcely be surprising if Lady Cowper instantly dismissed Emma as a
potential wallflower.

The moment she caught sight of her sister waiting
by the front door, however, Emma was reminded how
foolish she had been to worry about her own appearance. She was so cast in the shade by Georgiana's truly
dazzling beauty that no one, including Lady Cowper,
would spare her a second glance.

Georgiana was charmingly arrayed in a white muslin gown with the merest hint of lace edging the high
neckline and tiny puffed sleeves. Pink roses embroi-

dered around the hem were echoed by a silk flower
cunningly arranged in the blond curls. The gown was
a work of art: The overall effect was one of youthful
innocence, but no male eye would fail to observe the
delicate bones, the slender waist and gentle swell of the
bosom, the soft lips and blushing cheeks. Emma was,
with great satisfaction, reconfirmed in her belief that
Georgiana was certain to be much sought after and
couldn't fail to secure an eligible match.

Aunt Helen indicated her approval of the appearance presented by her two nieces, and the three ladies
were handed into the waiting carriage by a footman.

Once settled on the comfortable leather seat, Aunt
Helen fidgeted for a moment before saying nervously,
"I'm sure I don't need to tell you girls again how important this visit is. You mustn't give Lady Cowper
any cause to take you in dislike. Not," she hastily
added, "that she's likely to. Although we aren't close
friends, Emily and I have been acquainted for more
years than I care to admit to, and she is far too good-
natured to be anything but kind. She *is* a high stick-
ler, however, but of course your manners are such that
they can hardly fail to please."

She rattled on in this vein, and Emma could see that
Georgiana was becoming progressively more frightened. Emma fancied, however, that her aunt's words
were aimed at her. Aunt Helen must be aware that
Georgiana was unlikely to open her mouth during the
entire visit unless absolutely required to make a response.

Emma wondered guiltily if she could possibly have
been observed by Aunt Helen when she came in,
windblown and disheveled, from her morning ride.
There was no doubt her aunt would have deplored

Emma's indulgence in that wild ride, although she would have been equally shocked to have overheard the freedom with which Emma had spoken to the earl. Emma determined that the episode would be a lesson; she wouldn't again allow her conduct to go so far beyond what was pleasing, no matter how provoked she was.

LADY COWPER was an attractive, pleasant woman dressed in a stunning gown of apricot figured silk. As Aunt Helen and she exchanged compliments, Emma saw that there was one other occupant of the room, another very attractive matron, somewhat more daringly arrayed. Her morning dress was cut rather low in the neckline, and the thin silk clung to a still very shapely figure. Aunt Helen immediately exclaimed, "Sally! How delightful to find you here!" Emma thought she detected some insincerity as well as a shade of dismay in her aunt's voice, however, but the moment the woman was introduced to the two girls Emma understood.

The selection of Lady Cowper as the patroness to approach for the desired vouchers had been carefully made. Besides being an acquaintance, Emily Cowper was known as an amiable woman, not subject to sudden whims or pets.

Sally Jersey, on the other hand, known to her intimates as "Silence" because of her nearly nonstop chattering, was of another character altogether. Lady Jersey could be nearly as censorious as the more dreaded Mrs. Drummond-Burrell, and in addition was given to taking startling likes and dislikes, often for quixotic reasons. Lady Brookings had once caustically observed that at least Mrs. Drummond-Burrell was sincere, while for Sally Jersey it was a case of "do as I say, not as I do," because she was famous as a great flirt. From several comments her aunt had made, Emma gathered that she was not an admirer of Lady Jersey, and certainly would not have chosen her to sit in judgment on her nieces.

Emma was amused to find that Lady Jersey's reputation as a talker was not inaccurate; she was already carrying on a lighthearted monologue. Their hostess kindly ushered the visitors to a sofa and inquired as to whether they would care for refreshments. Aunt Helen refused for them all, apparently fearing to spoil the pretty picture her nieces made by allowing them to open their mouths.

Emma offered her sister an encouraging smile, then glanced across the room to find Lady Jersey's gaze fixed upon her, and was startled and offended by the coldness of it. She suddenly felt rather like a cow at the Harrogate market. She was undeniably being sized up, and probably found wanting. Almost despite herself, her spine stiffened and her chin rose slightly as she returned Lady Jersey's look with a cool stare.

That lady's eyebrows rose in surprise, and Emma felt Aunt Helen stirring beside her in agitation.

Lady Jersey broke into a musical laugh. "At least the chit has spirit, Helen! Is this the one with the money?"

Emma intensely disliked being spoken about as though she were not even present, but she couldn't afford to offend a social arbiter as powerful as Sally Jersey, so she maintained her silence.

Her aunt responded coolly. "Yes, Emma is fortunate enough to have been Lady Brookings's heiress.

Of course, Georgiana has a respectable portion as well.''

After shifting her gaze for a moment to Georgiana, who was blushing and keeping her eyes modestly lowered, Lady Jersey commented, "She won't need it, not with those looks! Fortunately, because if Denton's reputation is anything to go by, her portion will long since have passed over a gaming table!''

Emma bristled on her father's behalf, feeling it was none of this meddling busybody's affair how much money either daughter possessed, or whence it came. Anxiety fairly radiated from her aunt, however, so Emma merely said, "I am not conversant with Papa's finances, but I plan to increase Georgiana's dowry from my own inheritance." It was all very well to say Georgiana's extraordinary good looks would be enough, but there was an abundance of beautiful girls, and if word spread that she was a pauper, many men would seek elsewhere for a wife.

Mrs. Barlow said, "I don't think Harry would be so shabby as to spend the girls' dowries, although, thanks to Lady Brookings, for Emma at least the matter is irrelevant." Attempting to turn the conversation into more innocuous channels, she said, "My nephew has come to town for the season also. Charles has turned into a handsome young man."

Lady Jersey shrugged. "No one denies the Dentons have looks." Her gaze rested speculatively on Emma again for a moment; then she unexpectedly smiled with genuine warmth. "I don't think you're cut from the same cloth as your father, in any event. More like your mother, perhaps, although I don't believe I had her acquaintance."

Heaven forbid that resemblance, thought Emma, remembering her poor mama's indecisive, wishy-washy ways.

"I think you'll do very well for yourself," Lady Jersey continued, "although, of course, you'll have every fortune hunter in town running after you, so watch out! And it certainly won't do to attempt to outstare every lady you fancy has been impertinent to you. It's they who issue the invitations, remember, not the handsome young men."

Emma managed an apologetic, "It was rude in any case, ma'am. I fear I've been buried too long in the country."

"Not to worry! You have enough countenance to carry it off, so long as you don't go beyond the line. Tell me, can your sister talk?"

Emma nearly nudged her sister in the ribs with her elbow, but managed to refrain. Surely Georgiana had manners enough to make a suitable response, no matter how terrified.

Blushing furiously, the younger girl looked up and said, "Yes, indeed, ma'am. It's a pleasure to make your acquaintance." Her voice was little more than a whisper, but it sufficed.

Lady Jersey nodded with satisfaction and exchanged a long, thoughtful look with Lady Cowper, after which she said, "Your nieces will undoubtedly enliven the season, Helen. It will be a pleasure to watch all the young sprigs and the old fools scramble over themselves chasing these two, the one for her money and the other for her looks." She turned a surprisingly kind smile on Emma. "You'll find some who will want you for other reasons, I feel sure, so don't despair! You're not bad-looking, and a few men want some gumption in their wives, although not many." She turned back to Mrs. Barlow. "Anyway, we'll send the vouchers along. I'm having a ball next week, and I fancy you'll have received an invitation. Bring the girls, and your nephew, too, naturally."

The conversation then turned to indifferent subjects, and a few minutes later they were able to make their excuses and leave, feeling no small amount of relief.

In the carriage, Georgiana asked, "Aunt Helen, is everybody really going to be so interested in how much we're worth?"

She nodded. "Yes, and Sally was quite right about the fortune hunters, so you must be guided by your uncle and me on that. It's most vexatious, although it does ensure that neither of you will lack for escorts!"

Emma had expected her fortune to arouse interest, but even she had been somewhat surprised by the blunt inquiries. It appeared that word of her inheritance had traveled before her, which explained the flattering circle of young men who had surrounded her on the ride in Hyde Park. They had likely been forewarned by gossip that Max Barlow's niece was the possessor of a sizable fortune, and had been lying in wait for her, with no particular interest in her appearance or character. She briefly wondered whether the Earl of Ware might fall into the same category; his distinguishing attentions had evidently been quite out of character for him. She realized immediately, however, that her uncle would be aware if the earl had suddenly lost what was apparently quite a large fortune and needed an heiress, so she concluded that his attentions had been no more than they seemed: a mark of respect for his old friend, Max Barlow.

During the following week, Emma rode several times in the early morning, accompanied by a groom, and once by her uncle. She did not again encounter the Earl of Ware and might have thought him absent from London, except that several times Uncle Max mentioned something the earl had said the evening before at one of the clubs. Emma speculated on whether the man was a gamester, but finally decided not: Uncle Max had too much admiration for him.

The round of morning calls continued, and Emma was beginning to think she must have made the acquaintance of every hopeful mama and young lady in London, but had scarcely clapped eyes on anything male. Her aunt assured her, however, that once the season truly began, they would scarcely have time to draw a breath, and might remember this time of peace with nostalgia.

THE FIRST EVENING EVENT they were to attend was a musicale at the home of the Dowager Countess of Fincham, who was introducing a young daughter to the notice of society. The entertainment was to be provided by a succession of young ladies, all eager to display their talents. The countess had solicited Emma and Georgiana to perform, but then displayed a noticeable lack of eagerness, particularly, it seemed to Emma, when the countess considered Georgiana. No doubt she was far from eager to draw attention to such a stunning young lady, particularly since the contrast with her own plain daughter was so unfortunate. Emma was grateful to be able to excuse herself, and Georgiana, who was not musical, did the same.

Emma had a pleasant feeling of anticipation as, in the wake of her aunt and uncle, she entered the Fincham town house on the appointed evening. Georgiana was shrinking at her side, but immediately became more animated when Julia Hartley appeared from the crowd.

Julia politely greeted the Barlows, then expressed her delight that Georgiana wasn't to perform, either.

"All the better, anyway!" she insisted. "We'll be much freer to talk to people. Do come and meet my brother," she added, pointing to a handsome young man who gave every appearance of being desperately bored with the young lady who held him in conversation. "I'd love to have you for a sister-in-law, although I don't suppose you'll like John any better than I do."

Aunt Helen gave her permission, and the two girls made their way toward the young man, who had the same dark hair and eyes as his sister, although from a distance he appeared to lack her vivacity. Emma was quick to note the turned heads that followed their progress, especially male heads. The two girls easily outshone all the other young ladies present.

Emma surveyed the crowded rooms, but didn't detect the one particular dark head she sought. She was annoyed to find she was disappointed, but couldn't seem to prevent herself from looking up as each new arrival appeared in the doorway. Finally she casually asked her uncle, "Does the Earl of Ware not care for music?"

"On the contrary! He's very fond of it, and hasn't any reason to subject himself to one of these evenings! It would be a different matter if the young ladies had any musical talent, Emma, but they don't. You'll soon see what I mean. Ah, Linley," he said, turning to greet a man who appeared at his side, "I'm surprised to see you here! Didn't think this was your style."

"It's not," the other man said succinctly. It was clear to Emma that he hadn't noticed her, standing on the far side of her uncle. "I have a young cousin performing. My mother is bringing the girl out and asked for my escort. She's got a passable voice, but I'd be willing to wager she's the only one."

The man was attractive in a quiet way. Emma guessed him to be around thirty. He was quite tall and very thin, with a somewhat large nose, but he had a charming smile and a pair of very fine gray eyes that regarded her, as Uncle Max tucked her arm through his, in an interested fashion.

"Emma, I'd like you to meet Mr. Frederick Linley," he said. "Linley, my eldest niece, Emma Denton."

"It's a great pleasure," the man said, bowing over her hand. "Dare I hope to hear you perform this evening?"

Emma laughed. "I fear it's too late to retrieve yourself. I wouldn't dare now admit to any such intention!"

"And here I was just planning to offer to turn the pages for you. May I procure some refreshments instead, to make up for my abominable rudeness?"

"You're very kind, but I believe I'll wait. See, they're ready to start."

And indeed a young lady, dressed entirely in white, was arranging herself before a harp. It was obvious she fancied herself as presenting an angelic appearance, and, as Aunt Helen murmured in an undertone to Emma, the effect was spoiled only by the mediocrity of her playing.

"And," added Mr. Barlow, who had overheard the comment, "by the lack of wings!"

Unfortunately, this tedious performance was followed by another, and still another. By the time the refreshment break was announced, Emma was in complete sympathy with the Earl of Ware's desire to avoid such affairs.

She sipped a glass of lemonade brought her by Mr. Linley and exchanged polite chitchat with some of the ladies whose acquaintance she had made, as well as with several gentlemen whom her aunt brought to her notice. None were as handsome or as interesting as Mr. Linley, however, so Emma was pleased that he scarcely left her side and then asked permission to call on her.

She saw that Georgiana was surrounded by young men as well, and appeared to be enjoying herself, although she was allowing Julia to dominate the conversation, and it was Julia's tinkling laugh that could be heard some distance away. Nonetheless, there seemed to be quite as many gentlemen interested in Georgiana as in Julia, so Emma was well content.

In the carriage on the way home Aunt Helen sang Mr. Linley's praises. "Most eligible! No title, of course, and he hasn't Ware's looks, but very well off, and so charming! He's not given to flirtations, so it was quite encouraging that he singled you out so markedly. Did you like him?"

"Yes, I thought him pleasant," Emma said temperately.

Her aunt nodded with satisfaction before saying to Georgiana, "Despite what Julia says, her brother, too, is a very eligible *parti*. What did you think?"

"He was very nice," Georgiana said, but Emma, closely observing her sister, couldn't detect any sign that she felt even the tiniest flutter of the heart for the handsome Mr. Hartley. Perhaps she would come to, because there was no doubt that Lord Hartley's heir would suit her sister: He was handsome, young enough to be companionable and wealthy enough to support her in a comfortable style. What's more, Emma had seen the expression on his face as he looked at Georgiana when bidding the party good-night: he was moonstruck.

For herself, Emma regarded meeting Mr. Linley as the only high point in a very boring evening. She greatly feared that she had gone with the expectation of encountering Lord Ware and had allowed disappointment to color her attitude. Why she should care to see him at all was a puzzle to her, since he appeared to bring out the worst in her nature. Emma told herself that she was no longer a silly young girl and was too old to allow her head to be turned by a pair of stormy blue eyes!

The following morning the Barlow salon was crowded with young gentlemen, all eager to further their acquaintance with the dazzling Miss Georgiana Denton. Emma could see that her aunt was annoyed with her sister, and she felt no little irritation herself, for the younger girl had gone for a walk, accompanied by Julia and her maid, and been so late returning that the gentlemen had been forced to wait while she changed, although of course they were not informed as to the reason for the delay.

Julia and Georgiana had, in the past week or so, formed the habit of walking together each day, when their other engagements allowed it. Emma had no doubt at whose instigation this had come about; Georgiana had never been fond of exercise in any form, except perhaps dancing, but she made no demur at these daily excursions. Julia's maid was free to accompany the girls, so Aunt Helen considered it suitable.

The girls very properly invited Emma to accompany them, but she had no wish to intrude on their girlish confidences. They often returned from these strolls flushed and giggling, and she felt sure her presence would have a dampening effect. She suspected that, at present, all the confidences were on Julia's side; as yet, Georgiana had met so few young men and displayed no particular interest in any of them. The fact that Georgiana had felt no partiality for any of the young men present at the musicale, however, did not excuse her conduct today; common civility demanded her presence to greet morning callers.

Although several of the callers were amiable to Emma, she had no delusions that they were interested in her. She had not expected to be a social success, or to attract a great many gentlemen, and her first consideration was to find an eligible husband for Georgiana, but she was female enough to be pleased when Mr. Linley was announced by Tompkins, the Barlows' stuffy butler. Although the conversation remained general, Mr. Linley stayed at Emma's side throughout the visit and offered several very flattering compliments.

After the gentlemen had left, Emma noticed Georgiana appeared rather pale. She thought that perhaps the late night, coupled with the early-morning walk, had tired the younger girl. "Did you enjoy yourself?" she queried.

In a stifled little voice, Georgiana said, "Oh, Emma, I don't know what to say to them! It's so easy for Julia, and you looked so comfortable with Mr. Linley, but I . . . I have no conversation that would interest London beaux!"

"You had no difficulty conversing with Augustus Wenley, or Justin Broome, or—"

"That was different! They were just . . . just boys!"

Privately, Emma thought most of the callers today had been just boys as well. The talk appeared to consist almost entirely of boasts about each gentleman's proficiency in the hunting field, or with a pistol. Aloud she merely said, "These gentlemen are very little older and, in any case, are so entranced with you that you could probably say anything, or nothing, and they would be delighted! I saw no sign that the conversation lagged."

In her tiresome way, Georgiana simply repeated stubbornly, "You don't understand."

"We do understand, dear," Aunt Helen said in a kindly fashion. "But I think you will find that people are far less frightening when they're no longer strangers. In a month's time you'll doubtless laugh at yourself for being afraid. You'll have so many friends you'll feel quite at home."

Although this rallying speech produced a faint smile, and Georgiana murmured, "I'm sure you're right, Aunt," in an acquiescent tone, her color didn't improve, and she soon afterward made her excuses and retired to her room to rest.

Emma watched her sister leave the room, then sighed. "I fear I'm not as patient as I should be, but I must confess I find her timidity exasperating!"

Her aunt smiled. "I feel sure all we need is to have a little patience with Georgiana. How can so much attention from handsome young gentlemen fail to please? Once she discovers they have no desire to listen to witty discourses from a pretty girl, and in fact would prefer an admiring silence, she'll begin to enjoy herself as she ought. And, of course, dancing is a good deal more pleasant for a young girl than being in an overheated salon listening to dissonant music."

Emma felt there was a good deal of intelligence in her aunt's words and was persuaded she was right. Georgiana did enjoy dancing and, despite her shyness, had always been eager to attend the assemblies in Harrogate. Tonight's ball at Lady Jersey's would be the true beginning to the whirl of gaiety, and Emma, at least, was greatly looking forward to it.

CHAPTER FOUR

EMMA WAS SECRETLY RELIEVED when Charles and Cousin Alex, properly attired for a formal ball, presented themselves to dine at the Barlows' that evening. Emma had suspected that, if offered the opportunity to join some festivity promising more excitement, Charles would conveniently forget his promise to lend support to his sisters. Georgiana had remained shut in her room all afternoon with, she claimed, a slight headache and, although she had appeared in the drawing room before dinner, was still pale and subdued. Emma felt in need of reinforcements. Something or somebody was clearly needed to stiffen Georgiana's wilting courage.

The Barlows' town carriage was large enough to accommodate the entire party, and Charles's presence did seem to have a bracing effect on Georgiana, so that by the time they arrived at their destination the younger girl's cheeks were touched with pink and she actually laughed at one of Cousin Alex's sallies.

Mr. Linley materialized at Emma's side almost as soon as they entered the ballroom.

"You're beautiful tonight," he said simply as he took her hand.

"You've very kind," Emma murmured. She was slightly taken aback by the fervency in his voice. She suddenly realized she was going to have to consider him in the light of a suitor, and the thought made her uncomfortable. She liked him very well, but she had been so certain that no one would be interested in her, except possibly some fortune hunters, that it was now difficult for her to consider such a possibility seriously.

She *was* pleased at her appearance. Her looking glass had told her that the deep amber taffeta of her gown was flattering to the warm tones of her skin and showed the dark honey color of her hair to the best advantage.

She allowed Mr. Linley to claim the first dance, a boulanger, and once involved in the intricacies of the steps was unable to look about, but a quick glance showed her Georgiana being led out by John Hartley.

After Mr. Linley had restored her to her aunt, and departed with the promise of another dance, she had an opportunity to look around. The ballroom was draped with pink silk, and the effect was stunning, if a bit garish. Lady Jersey, of course, wore a gown of a deep rose color, which presented a striking picture against the silk-hung walls, but the ladies who had chosen to wear red or yellow were well advised not to allow themselves to be maneuvered into a position where their gowns made an unfortunate contrast.

"Here he comes!" her aunt hissed.

"Who?" asked Emma, but of course she knew. She looked in the direction her aunt indicated to see Lord Ware making his way through the clusters of people toward them. He was even more handsome than Emma had recalled. The severity of his well-cut black coat, combined with the elegant simplicity of his crisp white cravat, threw into relief the dark countenance, and especially the glittering blue eyes. He was a head taller than most of the other men, but his graceful carriage made them appear clumsy and out of proportion. Emma felt suddenly breathless, and to hide her disquietude she deliberately turned her head and pretended an interest in an attractive woman Charles was conversing with on the other side of the room.

"Mrs. Barlow, Miss Denton." His voice had a deep, husky timbre that cut through the babble around them.

Emma turned to look at him with feigned surprise. "My lord, how nice to see you." She hoped her tone was appropriately indifferent.

He inclined his head. "Your enthusiasm is heartwarming." There was laughter in his blue eyes, and for a giddy moment Emma had the feeling he was inviting her to laugh with him. When she didn't respond he went on, "May I have this dance?"

"I'm afraid not," Emma said insincerely. "I believe this is a waltz, and I haven't yet been approved by the patronesses." She was suddenly grateful for this social convention, which she had previously considered ridiculous. She was not at all certain she wanted to twirl about the room with the earl's large brown hand holding her waist.

One of his dark brows lifted smoothly, giving his face a sardonic cast. Coolly he remarked, "One tends to forget this is your first season." The blue gaze seemed to search out every incipient wrinkle and gray hair. Emma suddenly felt every inch the spinster. "May I have a later dance?"

Emma felt he was already glancing around for another partner. The music was striking up. "Certainly," she responded with equal politeness.

He put his name down for a country dance later in the evening, and then moved on with what Emma considered ungallant haste.

As the evening wore on, both Georgiana and Julia were constantly surrounded by a mob of young men who seemed prepared to indulge in fisticuffs at any moment for the privilege of leading their chosen lady onto the dance floor. Charles had done his duty by standing at Georgiana's side during the forbidden waltz and presenting to his sister those importunate gentlemen with whom he had become acquainted during his sojourn in London. From then on, Georgiana appeared to be in no need of assistance; there was no necessity to maintain a conversation on the dance floor, and between dances she had little to do but blush and disclaim any intention to favor one young man above another.

Emma was pleased to find herself a modest success as well. She was well aware that some of her triumph was a reflection of Georgiana's; well-bred gentlemen, when denied an opportunity to dance with the younger sister, felt obliged to hide their disappointment and turn with a semblance of eagerness to the elder Miss Denton. A number of her partners, however, were slightly older gentlemen who appeared to have no interest in Georgiana and who seemed to prefer to carry on a sensible conversation rather than to offer a stream of absurd compliments.

Mr. Linley had claimed the right to escort Emma to supper, and they joined a party made up of Lord and Lady Hartley, their son, John, who was escorting Georgiana, Julia, with the very handsome young Viscount Tennefoss, Uncle Max and Aunt Helen, and Charles, escorting the beautiful young woman with whom Emma had earlier observed him in conversation.

He presented her to Emma with an air of prideful possessiveness. "May I make known Mrs. Lydia Stonor? Mrs. Stonor, my sister, Emma."

Mrs. Stonor held out her hand with engaging formality. "Please call me Lydia."

Emma shook the proffered hand with restrained cordiality and said, "It's always a pleasure to meet any friend of Charles's. I hope you're joining us for supper?"

"Yes, indeed." Lydia placed a firm hand on Charles's arm. "Charles tells me this is quite a family party."

Charles interjected, "Mrs. Stonor is a widow, Emma."

Although this remark was certainly enlightening, Emma thought it was in poor taste, given the situation. As it was, she felt she had to murmur, "I'm so sorry."

A look that struck Emma as one of studied sadness crossed the lovely face. "Thank you, but it's been some time now. And we must put our sorrows behind us, don't you think?" Her dark eyes met Emma's with appeal.

"Of course I do," Emma agreed. "I'm sure that's what your husband would have wanted."

Lydia smiled with a tinge of satisfaction. "Oh, yes! Robert was the soul of generosity! I've told your brother all about him, haven't I, Charles?"

Charles's expression was tender as he looked down at the widow, and his tone was intimate as he murmured, "I'm only grateful that you've wanted to share your memories with me."

Emma's attention was recalled by Mr. Linley just then, but she was feeling very thoughtful as he seated her. Why had she felt such an instant dislike for Lydia Stonor?

The woman was beautiful, with smooth dark hair done up in a Grecian knot, velvety brown eyes with an almost Oriental slant, and a sleek body that moved with the boneless grace of a cat. She was attired in a wine-colored crepe gown, worn over a slip of rose sarcenet, that was immensely becoming, although it was a color that was not just then in vogue. Emma thought somewhat cattily that Mrs. Stonor would not dare wear the pale, clear shades currently in fashion, as they would surely make her skin appear sallow.

She was ashamed of her response to the woman. She feared her hostility was based on nothing more substantial than a reaction to the woman's undeniably exotic appearance. She told herself how absurd was her suspicion that Mrs. Stonor's apparent openness was false. She tried and failed to picture Lydia Stoner as the next Viscountess Denton, then had to chide herself. Would she have liked any woman her brother had presented in such a way? Emma had been mistress of Denton Hall for so long, perhaps it was natural to feel at least a twinge of jealousy for the woman who might prove to be her successor. Emma resolved to make an effort to be more friendly.

Her exertions on the dance floor had given Emma an appetite, so she was appreciative of the lavish spread. Mr. Linley procured her a plate with an assortment that included lobster patties and several jellies and ices. The conversation at their table was lighthearted and remained general. Although Emma couldn't seem to warm to Lydia, she was impressed with her demeanor, which was friendly without being forward, and always gracious. Emma only hoped, for her brother's sake, that the widow had a fortune to go with her apparent breeding, because Charles needed to marry money. It would be foolish for him even to dream of anything else.

Emma had paid little attention early in the evening to the parade of young men who were introduced to her aunt before being granted permission to dance with Georgiana, but shortly after the supper break she noticed a particularly handsome man who appeared slightly older than the others. His dark locks were arranged in a windswept style, and his swarthy good looks were enough to speed the heart of any young maiden. It was easy to endow him with swashbuckling propensities and imagine him as the hero of a popular ladies' novel. Emma also observed that at his appearance Georgiana's rosebud lips parted slightly, her breath seemed to come faster, and one white hand lifted to press her chest, perhaps to slow a leaping heartbeat.

Aunt Helen's eyes narrowed when she saw who was bowing over her hand. Her tone was decidedly unenthusiastic. "Georgiana, I believe you've met Sir James Finkirk." A warning glance accompanied the words.

Emma's interest sharpened. She recalled the dinner conversation when Mrs. Barlow had castigated Sir James as a gazetted fortune hunter.

Aunt Helen's warning went unheeded. Georgiana smiled sweetly. "Yes, it's very nice to see you again, sir."

His lips lingered on her hand. "May I hope for the pleasure of this dance?"

Georgiana blithely ignored the dozen gentlemen who had a prior claim. "Thank you, I'd like that." She rose and accompanied Sir James before anyone could register a protest.

Aunt Helen was not prepared to make a show of her annoyance before the whole world, so she forced an expression of pleasant indifference at the same time as she whispered to Emma, "How dare he barge in here like that and make off with her!"

Emma was thoughtfully watching her normally shy sister apparently chattering freely to the handsome man leading her through the steps of the country dance. "I don't think he made off with her," she said. "I'm afraid she went all too willingly. She acts as though she's known him forever!"

Aunt Helen sighed. "It must be that noble face. I don't know what Sally was thinking of to invite someone of his ilk this evening. I don't think there's a mother in the room who would want him dancing with her daughter."

Emma's gaze had not left her sister. "He's very handsome," she admitted. "Surely Georgiana's consequence won't be hurt by his indicating a preference."

"His reputation is too well known," Mrs. Barlow said flatly. "He isn't received in most houses anymore. Sally must just be indulging some quixotic whim!"

Emma's attention was claimed by two gentlemen wearing the striking uniform of the Hussars, but she found it difficult to turn her thoughts from her sister's disconcerting behavior. For Georgiana to be so disobliging as to ignore her aunt and uncle's express prohibition regarding the disreputable Sir James Finkirk was astonishing, especially for a girl so normally lacking in initiative.

Well, as Aunt Helen had said, they were not likely to encounter the man often, and there were so many dashing young men seeking Georgiana's favors that if she had formed some sort of *tendre* for Sir James on their brief acquaintance, it would soon be forgotten. All the same, she could only be relieved when Sir James restored Georgiana to her aunt's side and, without proposing a second dance or requesting permission to call, departed. Emma, seated only feet away, did not care for the intimate smile he gave Georgiana as he thanked her for the pleasure of the dance. Georgiana was immediately whisked away by another of the young men always waiting for an opportunity to stand up with her.

Just then Lord Rawdon arrived and eagerly solicited Emma for a second dance. Emma had met him earlier in the evening and had not cared for his glib compliments or the way he had of seeming to scan the room for a more advantageous prospect. She felt quite certain his family coffers were in disrepair.

If she hadn't found him so disagreeable, Emma would have been tempted to accept just for the pleasure of being unavailable when, and if, the Earl of Ware arrived to claim his dance. Although she had, of course, not specifically looked, Emma had not seen Lord Ware since he had vanished into an anteroom.

Lord Rawdon's smile, however, was so smugly confident that Emma found herself feeling annoyed. She made a production of hesitating, as though searching her memory, then said, "I believe…yes, I'm certain I promised this dance to the Earl of Ware."

Rawdon reached for her hand and said insinuatingly, "But as Ware doesn't seem to be here to claim this fair treasure...?"

Emma was searching for a suitably crushing reply when a deep voice interrupted. "Ware most certainly is." The earl had materialized at her elbow as though out of thin air. He held out his arm. "Miss Denton?"

Emma reluctantly placed her fingers on his forearm. Through the smooth black fabric of his coat she could feel the hard muscles, tensed as though he were restraining some strong emotion. Emma's fingertips tingled at the contact, and she felt unable to look into the earl's face.

Ware nodded at the other man with scarcely concealed coolness and said dismissively, "Rawdon." With that he turned, Emma at his side, and moved onto the dance floor.

Through the first movements of the dance Emma kept her gaze fixed on his waistcoat, a dark red figured silk. He made no effort to begin a conversation until Emma gathered her courage, lifted her chin and looked into the chilly blue eyes.

"Did your aunt approve your dancing with Rawdon?" he asked abruptly.

Emma answered icily, "I don't believe that's your concern."

"I'm a friend of your uncle's."

"As Uncle Max is here and quite capable of expressing his opinions to me, I repeat, I don't believe it's your concern."

Ware let out an angry breath. "Have you any idea...?"

Emma would have dearly loved to urge him to go on, as by now she was decidedly curious as to why he

considered Lord Rawdon so unsuitable. Surely it was
something more unsavory than mere fortune hunting,
of which half the men in London could be accused.
However, her pride would not allow it.

"I don't care to listen to gossip about my acquaintances," she said remotely.

With a disbelieving smile he said, "I had forgotten.
You make a point of ignoring reputations, don't
you?"

"To an extent," she agreed. "But, as I recall, what
I said to you was that yours is exaggerated in your own
mind, and that people have more interesting things to
talk about. It appears, though, that gossip about others as well as yourself does interest you to a remark-
able degree."

His brows had drawn together slightly. "That's impertinent, don't you think?"

Coolly she said, "The first impertinence was
yours."

She was startled when he threw back his head and
laughed, softening the forbidding lines of his face.
"You're never without an answer, are you?"

Emma, who was observing with fascination the tiny
indentation that had appeared in his cheek near the
corner of his smiling mouth, was naturally unable to
think of a single retort.

"I'm . . . I hope not," she finally faltered.

He chuckled again. "The music is ending," he observed. "Shall I politely return you to your aunt so
you can be marched out onto the floor again by some
bore, or shall we go outside and breathe a little fresh
air?"

"I'm sorry," Emma said, pulling her arm from his clasp and not meeting his eyes. "I think Aunt Helen would worry."

A disbelieving snort was her answer, but without further protest he escorted her toward the alcove in which her aunt was seated. Emma peeked at her companion, wondering if she ought to attempt to start a more conventional conversation to lighten the atmosphere. She sensed that he was disappointed, although whether it was in her, or simply because he had wanted to escape the overwarm air inside, she was not certain. She could not understand why he had sought her company when they so clearly struck sparks off each other. In silence they circled the crowded ballroom, to find that Uncle Max had joined Aunt Helen and that Georgiana was not dancing. Aunt Helen looked relieved on spotting Emma.

"Emma, Georgiana's headache has worsened. I think we should go home, if you don't mind?"

"Of course I don't," Emma returned warmly. "I'm sorry you're not feeling well, Georgiana. My lord," she said, inclining her head to the earl, "I'll wish you good evening now."

"If I might delay you for one moment," he said, smiling apologetically at Aunt Helen. "I've been hoping to make up a party to go to Vauxhall. I believe the Kinleys' ball is this week, but perhaps the following Saturday? I'd like you and your nieces to join me. And, um..." He glanced around, seemingly for inspiration. "And perhaps Lady Hartley and her charming daughter. And Linley, would you care to join us?"

It was obvious to Emma that he was hatching this scheme on the spur of the moment, that five minutes before, he had had no such intention. The others were excitedly agreeing, and the party was being enlarged as arrangements were smoothly taken out of Ware's hands. Somehow Lord Tennefoss, who had not strayed more than a few feet from Julia all evening, was included, as were John Hartley and Charles and Lydia Stonor, coincidentally passing by. Even Georgiana's cheeks had taken on color, and she was joining in the plans with more animation than she had shown since Sir James had taken his leave.

Emma, however, watched with suspicion as the earl gravely agreed to every suggestion and managed to appear eager to entertain this very large family party. She saw that Uncle Max, too, looked first astonished, then amused, at Ware's part in promoting such an unlikely expedition. After a moment he said, "I believe I'll come along, too, if you'll have me."

Lord Ware looked blandly at his old friend. "Why not?"

Although Georgiana's headache had been nearly forgotten by this time, the Barlows with their nieces in tow finally made their departure. Charles and Alex planned to go on to some club later in the evening with friends, so the return trip in the carriage was at least less cramped.

The drive was rather silent, as Aunt Helen acted on her oft-expressed rule against discussing personal matters, which the coachman might overhear. Emma thought the precaution futile, as experience had taught her that servants always seemed to know everything anyway.

Once home, Emma reluctantly trailed her aunt and uncle into the blue drawing room. She sank onto a gold-damask-covered satinwood sofa, watching her aunt similarly dispose herself in an armchair while Uncle Max took up a stance in front of the white tiled fireplace.

Georgiana lingered in the doorway. One soft white hand toyed at her throat with the elaborate clasp that held her blue velvet cloak.

"Aunt Helen, Emma, if you'll excuse me, I believe I'll go on up to bed. My head..." She pressed her temple with the tips of her fingers in what struck Emma as a slightly theatrical gesture.

"Of course you're excused," Mrs. Barlow said sympathetically. "I'll have Mabel bring up a hot posset. Just one thing, dear, and then we won't need to trouble ourselves about it again."

Georgiana, who had begun to turn away, stopped, head bowed and face averted.

"I don't like to see you dancing with a man like Sir James Finkirk. I realize that your generous nature makes it difficult for you to believe any of your acquaintances capable of shabby behavior, but Sir James is notorious and has made no secret of his necessity for marrying well to pull himself out of dun territory. He's not likely to make you an offer once he understands that your portion is no more than modest, and even if he did, your papa would be certain to refuse him. And it can do your reputation no good to be seen with the man."

Hot color had risen in Georgiana's cheeks, and now she swung back to face her aunt, her eyes sparkling and her chin set at an unaccustomedly rebellious angle. "Surely it would have been discourteous to turn him down. And, anyway, if I refused to dance with every man that I had no intention of marrying, I would have few partners!"

This spirited rejoinder echoed Emma's own thinking and put her in greater sympathy with her sister than she might otherwise have been.

Surprising herself, she spoke up in Georgiana's defense. "There's truth in that, Aunt Helen. In any case, Sir James can't be that much worse than some of the others. Lord Rawdon, for instance."

"What do you know about Rawdon?" her aunt asked sharply. "I've heard nothing to his discredit, although I don't believe his income to be high."

It was Emma's turn to blush. "Perhaps I'm mistaken," she mumbled. "It was something Lord Ware said that made me think . . . But I may have misunderstood."

Uncle Max interjected quietly, "Very likely not. I don't like to repeat gossip, but there are some ugly rumors circulating about Rawdon, having to do with a tradesman's daughter." The implication was plain.

Georgiana said hotly, "And Lord Rawdon is received everywhere, and Sir James is not! It is unjust!"

"Perhaps it is," Aunt Helen said, her expression weary, "but the fact is that he is ineligible. I suspect it would be all too easy for you to forget that, Georgiana."

Georgiana's cheeks paled, and after a stricken moment during which she stared at her aunt, she ducked her head submissively and said in a small voice, "I . . . I am not sure how to go about cutting someone."

In her kindly way Aunt Helen said, "I know it's difficult. If the occasion should arise again, just thank him and say that you've already promised this dance. I don't think he would be so bold as to press the matter."

Emma felt sad that her sister's first blossoming of romantic love, if such it was, should be for such a man, but felt certain that the hurt would not be lasting. After all, Georgiana had only met the man twice, and that briefly.

Once in bed, Emma experienced difficulty in falling asleep. She had enjoyed the evening while it lasted, but now was left with several troubling reflections. She suspected that an offer would not be long in coming from Mr. Linley and was uncertain how she should respond. She liked him but was not in love with him.

More disturbing was the question of why the Earl of Ware had acted so oddly: quarreling with her one moment, then the next making up a party that seemed to have no other purpose than an inexplicable desire for her company. If she had a higher opinion of her own attractions she might have been tempted to believe he had conceived a *tendre* for her and was unsure how to advance it, but she knew she wasn't beautiful and that he could have chosen any of the parade of young girls presented since he had come of age. No, that explanation would not suffice; there must be another. Puzzling the matter over kept her tossing and turning for nearly an hour.

CHAPTER FIVE

EMMA HAD GREATLY anticipated the first assembly at Almack's, which officially opened the season. It was gratifying to know that both girls were assured of an enthusiastic welcome at this citadel of the ton, and that neither need worry about being a wallflower. She was unsure whether to be glad or sorry that the Earl of Ware would probably not be present.

On the appointed evening she hurried through her own dressing in order to supervise the completion of Georgiana's. For herself she had chosen a simple gown of moss-green Berlin silk, and her hair was smoothly wound into a French knot on the back of her head.

She arrived in Georgiana's room to find her sister's toilette nearly finished. Georgiana was dressed for the occasion in a gown of primrose muslin, with the neckline laced with a velvet ribbon and a velvet sash about the high waist. A strand of tiny pearls had been used to gather her silvery-golden curls atop her head, with another strand resting about her slender throat. With silk slippers peeping from beneath her skirts and her dainty hands encased in gloves, she made an angelic picture, all that Emma could have desired.

"You look lovely," she said sincerely. Accustomed as she was to her sister's beauty, there were still times such as this when she saw it as though for the first time.

Georgiana was studying her reflection in the looking glass. "Thank you, Emma," she murmured absently as she straightened the velvet sash. Then she turned from the glass and said with real warmth, but sounding somewhat startled, "Emma, you look beautiful!"

"Thank you," she said, touched by Georgiana's compliment. "But you know I can't hold a candle to you. And as Aunt Helen would say, all those mamas are going to be green tonight!"

"You shouldn't denigrate yourself so," Georgiana protested, her pretty brow creasing. "I think you're far more attractive than you're willing to admit. You have such an air of... Oh, I don't know, sophistication and poise, that draws the eye."

"Nonsense!" Emma said forthrightly. "Don't try to convince me that I'm a beauty, because it won't work. I've looked into my glass too many times."

Georgiana said unanswerably, "Tell that to Mr. Linley, or the Earl of Ware! They must find you beautiful. And, you know, I think being in London must agree with you. You look...different."

"Oh, pooh, it's nothing but a new wardrobe, which I must admit I am enjoying." She hesitated. "Georgy, are you enjoying yourself? Or would you rather I had let you stay home?"

The younger girl pursed her lips and gave serious consideration to the question. "No," she said at last. "Then I'd have never known what it was like, would I? And I'm glad we came for your sake, because you *are* happy here, aren't you, Emma?"

"Yes," Emma said wryly, "but you didn't exactly answer my question."

Nor did Georgiana, who gathered up her cloak from where it lay draped over a chair and moved toward the door with an abstracted air. The conversation was clearly over. It occurred to Emma, as she followed her sister, that for some time she had had the feeling that Georgiana was not being entirely frank with her. But perhaps it was healthier that she now had a friend of her own age to confess her innermost feelings to.

The Barlow party arrived at the assembly rooms in King Street in good time to be greeted by Emily Cowper as soon as they entered the ballroom.

"Helen, Max, how nice to see you. At least I won't have to introduce *you* to people! And the girls look delightful!" A kindly smile accompanied her words. "I imagine there will be a stampede in your direction as soon as the gentlemen get a good look."

Her words were very nearly prophetic, as Georgiana's admirers surrounded her almost at once and began boisterously competing for the privilege of dancing with her. It was immediately clear that Emma, too, would have no difficulty in filling her card. The only dances either girl had to sit out were the waltzes. This was no hardship, however, as both were surrounded by gentlemen during these breaks.

Emma was surprised during one such break to catch an unexpected glimpse of Lord Ware standing in the doorway to one of the anterooms, eyeing the gathering. The amusements that Almack's offered would surely seem tepid to such a man as himself. No high stakes were allowed in the card room, and Aunt Helen had assured the girls that the refreshments were indifferent.

A notable absence was Lydia Stonor. Emma found it difficult to believe the widow had not been able to gain entrée to the exclusive citadel; she had such an air of breeding and confidence, of *belonging*, that Emma had assumed her to be a member of the aristocracy. But after all, Emma realized, she knew very little about Mrs. Stonor. Uncle Max had not been able to offer any information, and had thought Emma was concerning herself prematurely. Well, most likely her absence meant no more than that she had chosen to attend another entertainment more to her taste.

Tonight confirmed Emma's suspicions as to the depth of Charles's feelings, however. He didn't even glance about at the young ladies who would have eagerly stood up with him, instead disappearing early in the evening into the card room. This was a change for him, as he had always enjoyed dancing, having a reputation in their own neighborhood as a young man who enjoyed feminine companionship. Apparently Lydia's more mature company had spoiled him for the chatter of the young misses who observed his disappearance with such disappointment.

Emma had just been restored to her aunt's side after a country dance, during which her partner had maintained a tedious monologue on the excellence of trout fishing in Scotland, when Aunt Helen murmured, "Oh, here comes Ware. Is your next dance with him?"

Emma studiously did not glance in the indicated direction. "No," she said, "I believe this is a waltz."

Just then Lady Jersey, who had approached unseen, touched Emma on the arm. "Is the waltz acceptable to you, Miss Denton? May I present Ware as a suitable partner?"

The earl had smoothly timed his arrival to coincide with Lady Jersey's, and now bowed over Emma's hand. "Miss Denton? May I have the pleasure?"

Emma knew it was not usual to grant permission to young ladies to waltz at their very first appearance at Almack's, and so she murmured a confused thanks to Lady Jersey and acceptance to the earl before allowing herself to be swept into his arms.

Feeling unaccustomedly shy, she kept her gaze lowered and concentrated on the steps, trying to block from her mind her awareness of the earl's proximity and the touch of his hand on her waist.

Their steps fitted together remarkably well and Emma began to relax and enjoy the dance. She was not at all disappointed in her first waltz.

"You dance beautifully," he remarked.

Beginning to feel confident that her feet knew what to do, Emma looked up to meet Ware's blue eyes. She was so close that she could see his thick dark lashes and a tiny white scar, no bigger than the end of her thumbnail, on his temple. She was very nearly hypnotized by his steady gaze, and felt unable to look away. The other dancers were no more than colorful blurs that swirled about them.

She managed to say foolishly, "This is my first waltz."

"It hasn't reached the wilds of Yorkshire yet?"

She smiled a little. "All of the young ladies in Yorkshire know how to do it, but to their great disappointment it is considered too scandalous to perform in public."

He smiled, too. "I'm not surprised," he said. "You, however, do not dance like a novice."

She could feel warmth seeping into her cheeks, and wondered why she should be flustered by such a casual commendation when she had found the more florid compliments that she had been offered all evening merely boring.

"Thank you," she murmured. "You dance very well, too."

"Thank *you*," he said gravely, amusement in his eyes. "Do you know," he added after a moment, his tone light, "that I had to use all of my considerable supply of charm to allow us to have this dance?"

Unable to hide her surprise, Emma said, "You mean it was you who persuaded Lady Jersey...?"

"Who did you think?"

"I didn't think anybody," she said. "I mean, I supposed she was just being kind."

"Sally? Kind? She'd be flattered that you think so."

Emma found herself feeling breathless. "I'm flattered that you exerted yourself so on my behalf."

"Not on yours. On mine. I wanted to dance with you."

His eyes had narrowed and held a disquieting gleam, while his fingers had tightened on her hand. Emma had to look away from his suddenly bright gaze and speak to herself very sternly. She mustn't read anything deeper into a flirtatious remark than was meant. Nonetheless, she could think of nothing appropriately lighthearted to say and after a moment the music ended.

As he accompanied her back to her aunt, the earl appeared so much his usual self that Emma almost believed she had imagined the tension she had felt in his touch and the intentness of his gaze. He parted from her with no more than a brief bow to her aunt, and a murmured, "Thank you for the dance."

Inexplicably, Emma felt as though the evening had just become a success.

IN THE NEXT WEEK, Emma became increasingly worried about Georgiana. Idly playing scales on the pianoforte one afternoon, she wondered if she had made a mistake in bringing her sister to London. They attended a constant round of exclusive entertainments: Venetian breakfasts, musicales and routs. Georgiana, dressed to perfection, followed without complaint wherever she was led and docilely went through the motions of dancing and holding court for her circle of admirers. There was no indication that she was enjoying herself in the least. Without the spark that could lend charm to her delicate features, she appeared like a beautiful doll that would be better placed on a shelf to be admired than played with. It seemed to Emma that some of Georgiana's beaux had transferred their allegiance already, and although it was to be expected that such young gentlemen might prove fickle, it was becoming obvious that the crowd about Georgiana had shrunk, while Julia Hartley's circle had, if anything, swelled. Her vivacity made an unfortunate contrast to Georgiana's unresponsiveness.

And it seemed to Emma unnatural that her sister didn't appear to notice or resent this contrast. In fact, the two girls were closer friends than ever, and their morning walks had become a fixed part of their routine. Emma could only be thankful for them; Georgiana obviously anticipated the walks with pleasure, and always returned home with better color in her cheeks and a sparkle in her eyes.

Emma was determined to finish out the season now that they were here and she had been put to such expense. She would have been in despair about Georgiana's chances of receiving a suitable offer at all, except that John Hartley's attentions had become marked. Although there was no indication that Georgiana had conceived a *tendre* for her friend's brother, she seemed to like him well enough and accepted his courtship with some complaisance.

Emma found these thoughts lowering, and of a sudden she was eager to be out of the house and doing something physical. The drive she had taken earlier in the day with Mr. Linley, although pleasant, had been no more tiring than would have been conversing in the drawing room. It had exercised her mind and tongue, while having no such effect on her limbs. Too many days were passing with no more physical exertion than such a drive afforded.

Emma gave a decisive nod and stepped out into the hall. "Betty!" she called to her maid, wishing she could have dispensed with her chaperonage. Betty was London-bred, and her idea of a walk was the distance from the carriage to the front steps.

With her maid scurrying behind her, Emma set off across the square at a brisk pace, determined to stretch her legs and blow some of the cobwebs from her mind. Perhaps she would take the opportunity to visit Hatchard's and select some new novels to while away idle moments. The absurd frolics of the heroines in popular novels were difficult to take seriously, but were excellent for lulling Emma to sleep when she felt as flighty as Caspar did when he had been too long confined. An evening spent fending off the advances of Lord Rawdon, at the same time attempting to divide

her attention equally between her other admirers
(while surreptitiously watching for the Earl of Ware to
make one of his infrequent appearances) could not be
considered relaxing.

At Hatchard's, Betty waited outside, watching her
mistress through the bow windows, which displayed
the newest books and magazines. Almost randomly
Emma chose several books and journals; at home she
had not had ready access to a lending library, and
Godmother held modern novels in low regard, so
Emma was unfamiliar with most of the authors and
had no need to await new publications eagerly, as did
most of the ladies.

The walk home was tiresome, enough so to make
Emma resolve to find another companion for her
strolls. Betty's steps lagged, and in a whiny voice she
several times complained of stones in her slippers. By
the time they turned the corner into Berkeley Square,
the maid was ostentatiously limping, suffering, she
insisted, from a bruised heel. Emma was out of patience and took the books from her. Now, with home
in sight, she allowed her pace to quicken. The square
was nearly deserted, with most of the occupants resting before the evening's entertainments, but Emma
idly noted a hackney waiting in front of a house several doors down from the Barlows'.

Emma shifted the books to her other arm and
glanced impatiently back to make sure her maid didn't
require assistance. She heard the crack of a whip and
the clatter of hooves on the cobblestones as the hackney started toward her. The coachman seemed to be in
a hurry, she thought, and wondered at his hasty departure. She had seen nobody come out of the house,
either to enter the closed carriage as a passenger or to

give the coachman a message. It was unusual, in this neighborhood of exclusive homes, to see a shabby coach for hire; residents of Berkeley Square were more apt to arrive home in a bright yellow barouche, with a coat of arms on the side, or in a sporting curricle, with a high-strung pair prancing in the harness.

Emma gave a mental shrug. Most likely the coachman had been instructed to wait for a message and had grown impatient. Emma was not even acquainted with the occupants of that particular house, so their doings could hold no interest for her. She looked once again over her shoulder and, seeing that Betty was hobbling pathetically along, stopped walking. She didn't want to abandon the girl altogether, just in case she should happen to stumble and turn her ankle. The maid was obviously more concerned about the effect her limp was having on Emma than about where she placed her feet.

When she saw Betty stop, a peculiar expression on her face, and begin to wave her arms, Emma was momentarily irritated, thinking this was some new stratagem on the girl's part to further convince her mistress of her suffering. Then she saw the fright in the girl's pale eyes and her mouth open in a scream that could hardly be heard over the pounding of the horses' hooves and the creak of the carriage.

Emma swung about just in time to see the horses, driven on by the snap of the whip on their backs, bearing down on her at a dead run. The moment was one of those that crystallized, to be recalled later in fantastic detail.

The horses were big brutes, perhaps part shire or Belgian, with enormous feathered feet, which pounded the earth with the force of thunder. Their powerful reddish-brown chests, streaked with sweat, filled Emma's horizon, and she was half mesmerized by the rolling eyes and foam-flecked muzzles. The man so mercilessly driving the panicked horses on was wrapped in a brown cloak, even his face shadowed from the gaze of chance onlookers.

Emma stood still for that frozen instant, expecting the horses to swerve from their path, but frantically aware all the while that such clumsy animals hadn't the agility of the leggy Thoroughbreds that could be driven with such precision by a member of the Four-in-Hand Club. This thought was no sooner in her mind than she reacted. Knowing, hampered as she was by her skirts, that she had no time to run, Emma dove to the side, landing with stunning impact on her right shoulder and then rolling. She felt a hot wind as the horses plunged past, and she instinctively pulled herself into a little ball.

She didn't move for a long while, not wanting to acknowledge the pain in her shoulder. Doubtless because of the shock, her mind was blank, even at peace. It was the very stillness that intruded at last. With a groan she began to draw herself up, clutching at her shoulder, which felt as though it had been wrenched from the socket. She saw her maid running toward her, all pretense of a limp abandoned.

"Miss! Miss! Did it hit you? Are you hurt? Shall I . . ." The expression on the girl's face changed as she took in Emma's appearance. "I don't think you should move, miss. Let me get help."

"No, no." Emma shook her head impatiently. "Give me a hand, Betty. The coach missed me, no thanks to the madman at the reins! I hurt my shoulder a little when I fell, but I can walk, if you'll help me. Aunt Helen would have a seizure if you went running in with some tale of my being injured!" She smiled weakly, more to reassure the doubtful maid than because she found any cause for humor in the situation.

She looked down at herself and saw that her muslin gown was torn in several places and had a streak of dirt down the side where she had landed. She put one shaking hand up to touch her face, wiped off the dampness she could feel, then held her hand out in front. It was not the wet of tears on her fingers, but dirty white foam from the horses' mouths, so close had destruction come to her.

Emma closed her eyes for a moment and took a deep breath, then opened them again and said steadily, "Let's start home, shall we? It's just a step. I'm sorry I dragged you out today, Betty. This walk has been ill-omened from the start."

"Yes, miss," the maid agreed with alacrity.

Their faltering arrival up the front steps produced all the excitement Emma had feared. The well-trained footman who swung open the door gave a gasp, heard by the butler. Tompkin's demeanor was normally so disinterested as to border on the inhuman, and under other circumstances it might have given Emma pleasure to see his eyes widen and his expression evince shock. In addition to the pain in her shoulder, however, Emma had just become aware that she had also skinned her knee, and probably her elbow as well, as both had begun to burn.

Just then the door to the blue drawing room was flung open and Aunt Helen burst out. "Emma, is that you at last? I've—Emma!" she cried in horror. "What happened? No, don't tell me! You shouldn't be standing!'' She bustled forward to take Emma's other arm and eased her toward the drawing room. ''Tompkins,'' she tossed over her shoulder, ''send for Dr. Bates. Have him come immediately!'' She ignored her niece's feeble protest. ''Here, lie down on the sofa.''

Emma was surprisingly exhausted by the effort she had made in walking home. She found her aunt's solicitude comforting, so without further argument she allowed herself to be led into the drawing room and, freeing her arms, sank onto the blue damask sofa. Her shoulder was throbbing and her hands had begun to shake and her teeth to chatter.

Betty immediately burst into her tale of the huge black coach drawn by monstrous brown horses that had flame leaping from their nostrils and thunderclaps echoing from each hoof. This image was not so very far from Emma's own recollection, but she repressed a shudder and said commonsensically, ''Please don't exaggerate, Betty. My aunt will be alarmed enough as it is.'' She shifted her gaze to her aunt, whose soft face was puckered with worry. ''I was nearly run down by a hackney with some fool at the reins who thought himself in a great hurry and paid no mind to who might be in his path! Thanks to Betty's warning, however, I was able to jump out of the way with time to spare and,'' she concluded, putting from her mind how close those great hooves and iron-shod wheels had come to her, ''the only damage done was to my shoulder in falling. And I believe I skinned my knee.''

Mrs. Barlow was regarding her skeptically, apparently not reassured by this prosaic recounting of the accident. "Where did this happen? Did you glimpse the man's face? He should be clapped behind bars!"

Emma frowned. "It was just a few feet from our door. And, no, I was unable to see his face, although I admit I was preoccupied with other matters. I'm sure it was a hired coach, and I first noticed it because it had drawn up in front of one of the neighbors'. It was shabby-looking, you see, and seemed out of place. It was at the house two doors down."

Mrs. Barlow promptly sent a footman to inquire into the identity of the mysterious coach. She seemed fired with a zeal to punish anyone who, even accidentally, should have endangered a member of her family. Emma had the brief thought that her aunt would have enjoyed a large brood of children.

By the time the doctor arrived, Emma was ensconced in her own bed, dressed in a warm nightgown to combat the chills she was feeling. Dr. Bates was fairly young, with a crooked nose and muddy, palely lashed eyes, but his long-fingered, bony hands were gentle and the examination scarcely hurt.

At length he smiled and said, "I think you have nothing worse than a wrench, which time will heal with no assistance from me. I predict your shoulder will be quite sore tomorrow, but greatly better by the next day, although it will doubtless be stiff for some time. And as for feeling chilled, that often occurs after an accident and is probably the body's way of assuring that you stay tucked in bed. I want you to stay warm and drink some hot milk with brandy in it. It will help you sleep, which will do you a world of good." He picked up his bag and prepared to depart. "Send for me again if you feel the need, but I'll be surprised by a summons. Miss Denton is young and healthy and will mend quickly.''

With the help of the hot milk and brandy, which warmed her within, Emma soon fell asleep and didn't wake until the next morning. As Dr. Bates had predicted, her shoulder ached abominably and was so stiff she could scarcely lift her arm. With Betty's help, however, she rose from bed and managed to get dressed. For once she was grateful that she now had her own maid, because she knew her aunt's dresser would have refused to assist and would have hurried to get Aunt Helen, who then would have insisted Emma stay in bed.

Indeed, Emma's appearance in the breakfast room was greeted with dismay. Aunt Helen dropped the pile of invitations she had been idly scanning onto the table, where they fanned out among the cutlery. Even Uncle Max's eyebrows went up in barely restrained surprise.

"Emma!" exclaimed Mrs. Barlow. "I'm sure you're not well enough to be about! Let me help you back to bed." She began to rise from her place at the table.

Emma calmly moved forward and sat down, trying to disguise how the movement pained her. "Good morning," she said. "Please don't fuss, Aunt Helen. My shoulder is somewhat stiff, but otherwise I feel fine, and you know I'd die of boredom cooped up in my room. I promise not to go out today. Will that satisfy you?"

Aunt Helen studied her doubtfully. "If you insist, Emma. I'll have Tompkins refuse any visitors as well, so as not to tire you." She anticipated Emma's protest. "A day of rest will do us all good. I fancy Georgiana has been looking a little peaked lately."

Emma applied herself to her breakfast, surprised to find her appetite intact. Aunt Helen was clearly reassured by the quantity of food she tucked away; it was the older woman's philosophy that when all was well with the digestive tract, little could be amiss with either the body or the soul. This was why she was frequently concerned about Georgiana, who had a birdlike appetite and barely ate enough to sustain herself.

Uncle Max pushed his chair back from the table and crossed his legs. "Emma," he said, his tone businesslike, "would it disturb you to discuss the accident? Your aunt is determined that an effort should be made to bring the malefactor to justice."

"To justice?" Emma looked her surprise. "I feel certain it was an accident. The man was undeniably careless, but surely talk of dragging him before a court of law is extreme!"

"Are you so certain it was an accident?" His eyes were intent. "Your maid thought it looked very much as though the horses were deliberately driven at you."

Emma laughed to hide her uneasiness. "And did Aunt Helen tell you Betty also thought the horses had flames coming from their nostrils? Betty is a nice girl, but very much disposed to see a monster around every corner! What possible reason is there to think the incident anything but an accident? I have no enemies!"

He nodded. "Nonetheless, it's odd. The coach was waiting in front of Lady Chartwell's, but she knows nothing about it. The butler was just going to send a footman out to tell the coachman to move along, or at least find out what he wanted, when he started up, so fast, the butler said, it was as though he had received a scare."

"Nonsense," Emma asserted. "He probably saw the butler looking at him through the window and realized he was going to be sent about his business with a flea in his ear. Perhaps whoever he was waiting for failed to make an appearance and he was annoyed. I'm sure it's no more than that."

Uncle Max accepted this explanation. "Very likely. Lady Chartwell has a young daughter, whose acquaintance you may have made. Perhaps she concocted some plans that didn't come to fruition, and doubtless thankfully so."

Aunt Helen had an arrested look in her eyes. "Are you suggesting Amanda Chartwell was planning an elopement? She's a silly young girl, but still...!" Her scandalized tone changed to one of pleasurable surmise. "All the same, it would certainly explain the entire incident. Perhaps she counted on her mother's being out, but then something went wrong and, naturally, with Lady Chartwell home she had no choice but to pretend nothing was going on. And the coachman was most likely her suitor..."

"He did have his face covered," Emma admitted, for once not averse to encouraging one of her aunt's fantasies. "I don't think he wanted to be recognized."

Aunt Helen nodded triumphantly. "The scoundrel! And so he did receive a scare! Amanda didn't appear, but he could see that he was being watched from behind the curtain. So he fled, and in his state of mind it's no great wonder he didn't see you!"

Emma could think of a few small holes in this story, such as the fact that the young Amanda Chartwell was unlikely to plan an elopement in late afternoon right under the eyes of a house full of servants. Nonetheless, the story was attractive and did explain a great deal. It might not be accurate in all of its particulars, but perhaps it contained enough of a kernel of truth to explain the incident. Emma had been conscious of a degree of disquietude, because, in the fright of the moment, it had seemed to her, too, that the coachman had had a malevolent purpose. Now she realized how absurd such a fancy was, and her mind felt at rest.

She was so grateful to her aunt that she wasn't even annoyed when Mrs. Barlow said suddenly, "Are we going to have to cry off tomorrow? We don't want Ware to think you're not flattered by his invitation. And Vauxhall is so romantic! This could be the ruin of all our hopes."

Emma exchanged rueful smiles with her uncle. "Aunt Helen," she said patiently. "I *have* no hopes where the Earl of Ware is concerned. However, should I have to stay home, I see no reason to believe he wouldn't accept my explanation. He's not going to be looking for an insult where none exists."

Aunt Helen looked disappointed. "It never pays to allow a promising moment to pass by unused. It might make him skittish, and reluctant to commit himself for another evening."

Emma rolled her eyes. "Aunt Helen, the Earl of Ware is not a horse! And he doesn't allow skittishness in his mount, so I doubt he would permit any behavior in himself that could be labeled such. However, I see no reason to believe I won't be restored tomorrow, just as Dr. Bates said. I won't need to ride a horse, or dance, which might strain my shoulder. I feel sure I'll be strong enough to enjoy an evening at Vauxhall.''

CHAPTER SIX

EMMA WAS THE FIRST to alight from the carriage, glancing curiously as she did so through the open gate to the river. The earl bowed briefly over her hand, but then turned promptly to assist Aunt Helen in negotiating the steps. Emma saw that the Hartleys' carriage had stopped just behind the one she had descended from, and that Lord Tennefoss was already handing Julia down.

Although it was a warm evening, the river seemed to be acting as a funnel for a brisk breeze, so that as Emma walked out onto the small stone jetty she pulled her cloak more tightly about her shoulders. Two boats were tied, bow and stern, to the jetty, and their high, curving prows swayed and dipped with the currents. The boatmen waited patiently over their oars.

Emma had been surprised when the earl suggested the party make their approach to Vauxhall by water. The notion seemed to suggest an unsuspected streak of romanticism lurking in his breast. Whatever his motive, however, she was greatly anticipating the boat ride, as she had never been afloat on any body of water, large or small, and was eager for the new experience.

Lydia Stonor and Charles were the first to follow Emma onto the jetty, the widow with her hand resting lightly on Charles's arm.

"Miss Denton. How delightful to see you again! It was so clever of Lord Ware to suggest this outing. I've never been to Vauxhall before, have you?"

"No, I haven't," Emma admitted. "This is my first visit of any length to London."

To her surprise, Lydia confided, "Yes, mine, too. It's difficult, not knowing many people, don't you think? Although you've had your aunt and uncle's guidance."

Was Lydia's tone wistful? Emma wondered. But surely she had some sort of sponsorship, else how had she secured an invitation to Lady Jersey's? Emma's agreement was heartfelt, however. "Yes, and I'm grateful for it. They've been so kind."

This sort of conversation, innocuous and loaded with platitudes, would once have bored Charles to death, but now he merely smiled fondly at Lydia and momentarily covered her hand with his. "Are you warm enough?" he inquired.

"Yes, thank you, Charles. Although I'm glad for the cloak."

He glanced belatedly at Emma. "Emma? But I know you're accustomed to a chill wind! I daresay the snow has scarcely melted off the hills at home."

Emma felt a tiny pang of homesickness, although not for the snow. Still, the steep fells of Yorkshire, cloaked with heather and grass, were at their most beautiful in the spring. The gentler landscape here in southern England had its own attraction, but left Emma feeling somewhat hemmed in.

By this time the party had gathered on the jetty and was prepared to embark. As Emma stepped down into the frail craft, it swayed alarmingly under her added weight, and she sensed the current's insistent tug. Mr.

Linley made haste to claim the seat next to Emma, while the earl, displaying no perturbation, sat comfortably in the middle. Georgiana had chosen to join the other younger members of the party in the second boat under Lady Hartley's benign chaperonage.

Knots were quickly untied and the two boats slipped smoothly out into the dark waters of the Thames. Few other boats were moving about so late, but they passed near a number of anchored ships, whose black silhouettes and forests of rigging rose far above them. Lanterns, fastened to rails and prows, cast their feeble yellow light on the water, where it danced with the ripples and then was swallowed by the inky river. The moon was a mere sliver, and lent no illumination to the scene.

Emma leaned far enough over the side to let one hand trail in the chill water. The oars moved without a splash, cutting cleanly on each stroke, scarcely disturbing the surface. Nobody in Emma's boat spoke, their silence attesting to the fairyland beauty of the river at night, so different from the bustling commercial highway it was during the day. Lydia's expression was one of bemusement as she glanced about, and Charles's equally so, although for different reasons; his gaze remained fixed on his lady. Emma avoided looking at Ware's shadowed face, but she had the uncomfortable impression that he was watching her.

They arrived all too soon at the gaily lit entrance to Vauxhall Gardens, and Emma reluctantly found herself with her feet back on earth again as the boats vanished into the darkness. At first glance the gardens were charming, with lawns and walkways reaching down to the river. An outdoor concert was in progress, and the melancholy strains of Mozart laid a subtle counterpoint to the holiday spirits so in evidence on the visitors' faces.

The earl said, "I've reserved a box for supper. We can hear the music from there."

The box, somewhat larger than those in a theater, as well as being outdoors, was just able to accommodate their party. Its gilded front looked out on a promenade, so that one could exchange greetings with passing acquaintances, and it was squeezed between two other boxes, one occupied by a family group similar to their own, and the other by two couples.

The gentlemen in this box had clearly partaken of too much punch and, more shockingly, the women acted as though they, too, were inebriated. They were allowing themselves to be cuddled in an intimate fashion, and were giggling and squirming closer to their gentlemen friends. A very brief glance sufficed to assure Emma that, although quite pretty, they were not ladies; their thin muslin gowns were cut immodestly low, and one wore an enormous ruby pendant that nestled in the valley between her vulgarly displayed breasts.

Mrs. Barlow hesitated before entering their own booth. She glanced from her nieces to the couples in the other box and was obviously waging an internal struggle. The attractions of Vauxhall won, as she finally let her nieces pass and found a seat herself. Emma saw that Georgiana was blushing furiously, while Julia was sneaking fascinated peeks at the two women. Lady Hartley entered the box close behind her daughter and hissed into her ear, just loudly enough that Emma overheard, "Try for a little conduct! A *lady* doesn't stare!" She might have pointed to Lydia Stonor for an example; the shocking couples might as well not have existed for all the notice the attractive widow gave them.

Emma was intrigued by a brief byplay between her and Charles, however; her brother glanced at the other box and then at Lydia with raised brows, evidently asking her if she would prefer to leave. The dark-haired woman simply gave a faint smile and slight shake of the head, and Charles's expression indicated that he would accede to her wishes. Emma had never liked her brother so well; Lydia might be difficult to warm to, but she was surely having a positive effect on Charles, for which his sister could only be grateful.

Emma found herself between Mr. Linley and Lord Ware. Mr. Linley leaned forward to address Ware loudly, his tone slightly aggressive. "Perhaps another box could be found? This is a disgraceful sight for the young ladies. I won't have them offended!"

Mrs. Barlow took umbrage at his well-meant high-handedness. Before the earl could respond, she said coolly, "I think Lady Hartley and I are quite capable of determining what is permissible and what is not! We knew before coming that one must take the bad with the good at Vauxhall."

Mr. Linley's sandy brows rose at her sharpness, but she had left him with no retort. Finally he glared at the other box and muttered "Young puppies!" before turning to respond courteously to a bid for attention from Julia, who sat at his other side and who seemed determined to gain the notice of all of the gentlemen, except, of course, her brother.

The earl said in a low tone, as he held Emma's gaze, "*Do* they offend you? I'll get rid of them if you like."

Emma glanced at the other box just in time to see one of the men dip his hand into the bodice of the woman's gown, his fingers brushing the mounds of white flesh, and pull out the ruby, which glowed in the bright light like a hot coal. The woman giggled and turned toward the man, pressing her breasts against his coat.

Emma lowered her gaze in confusion and murmured, "No, no, they don't bother me. I...I was just admiring...what a fine ruby necklace."

"Very fine," the earl agreed dryly. "And costly. Are you wishing you possessed one like it?"

"Thank you, but no," she said with composure.

"Don't thank *me*," he said offensively. "I didn't offer you one!"

Emma gave him as icy a look as she could muster, then showed him her shoulder as she turned to converse with Mr. Linley.

The other party was soon forgotten as their own group was served a supper of the peculiar delicacies Vauxhall was known for: powdered beef, custards and syllabubs laced with wine. The gentlemen accepted glasses of arrack punch, while the ladies sipped lemonade. Spirits were high; the older members of the party maintained an animated conversation and called occasional greetings to passing friends, while Julia carried on an outrageous flirtation with Lord Tennefoss right under her mother's nose, and John Hartley hovered solicitously over Georgiana, attending to her every want. It seemed to pass unnoticed that Emma was ignoring Lord Ware, who in turn appeared unconcerned by her rebuff.

She wondered at his offer to rid them of their neighbors. If she had expressed such a wish, would he have coolly evicted them? It was easy to picture Mr. Linley blustering to no purpose at the foursome, while the earl would doubtless have succeeded in hastening their departure by a quelling look and a few blistering words.

She could only suppose he had intended his other remarks in jest, but she found his implication that she had been hinting for a similar jewel offensive indeed. His words had had a certain bite to them, as though he had too often had lady friends beg for such baubles. Did he think her no better than the light-skirts with whom he was apparently more accustomed to keeping company?

His husky voice brought her out of her reverie.

"I believe there is to be a fireworks display at midnight. If anybody would care to take a stroll, perhaps we should do so now."

It soon developed that everybody wanted to see more of the gardens, although some were more eager than others. Lady Hartley looked as though she would have liked to put Julia on a leash, and her object in taking a walk was clearly to keep her eye on her daughter. Georgiana accepted the young Mr. Hartley's arm with every appearance of enjoyment. The earl offered his arm to Emma and, after the briefest of hesitations, she rested her hand on it. She had no wish to draw notice to the awkwardness between them, and she could see no danger in walking with him for a short way. Their group would no doubt stay together, and she could shortly find some opportunity to exchange partners with Lady Hartley, who had taken Mr. Linley's courteously proffered arm.

The paths were hung with brilliantly colored lamps, which seemed to be more for effect than for real illumination. Much of the way was quite dark, and other paths branched off the one they were following. To no

one's surprise it took Julia and Lord Tennefoss only
a minute to vanish, with Mr. Hartley and Georgiana
following only a moment later.

Lady Hartley's lips pursed in vexation, and she
called sharply, "Julia! Julia, where are you?" When
there was no response she began to look agitated, and
after calling again to no avail, quickened her steps,
drawing Mr. Linley with her.

Emma thought her quest hopeless; she had noticed
several benches placed behind thick shrubbery, and
with the number of intersecting paths the possibilities
for escaping detection were limitless. Aunt Helen
seemed less concerned about Georgiana's disappearance, understandably so since she shared Emma's
conviction that John Hartley would make an admirable husband. All the same, she and Uncle Max hurried to keep up with Lady Hartley, perhaps out of
sympathy. Charles and Lydia, too, stayed with the
others, although Emma thought her brother looked a
trifle aggrieved. Emma understood Lydia's thinking
very well, however; as a young, attractive widow, she
had to take great care to protect her reputation.

The earl's unhurried pace, and perforce Emma's,
did not change. "I believe they've lost their charges,"
he remarked calmly. "No sense hunting. They'll show
up in their own good time."

Although this echoed her own earlier reflections,
Emma was unreasonably annoyed by this evidence of
the earl's lack of concern.

The older members of the party became lost to sight
around a bend in the path. Emma's hand was firmly
imprisoned between Ware's arm and his body, holding her captive. When she tugged to free her hand, his
arm tightened, reminding her again that his relaxed,

unhurried manner and fashionable garments hid a powerfully muscled body.

She stopped dead in the path and glared at him. "Please release my hand!" she said sharply.

His brows rose in exaggerated surprise, and he said, "Certainly."

The moment her hand was freed Emma hurried forward, uneasily conscious of the darkness and of the earl following close behind. When she came around the bend in the path she discovered the way forked, and nobody else in sight. There seemed nothing to choose between the paths, and she had no idea which way to go.

Ware's strong fingers gripped her elbow, as though he were reclaiming possession, and he said, "I believe this left path circles back toward the river. I think it the likeliest way."

It suddenly occurred to Emma that it was the earl who had engineered this outing, as well as suggesting the walk, and it might very well be that matters had come out just as he had intended them. It was this suspicion, along with an inexplicable perversity, which made her say stubbornly, "I think the right way is more promising."

He simply shrugged. "Whichever you prefer."

Emma was by no means certain of her choice and was somewhat disappointed that he had not argued, thus shoring up her own conviction. They began to walk again, but encountered no one. It seemed to Emma that this path was even darker than those they had left behind, and she began to wish she had not allowed her feeling of antagonism to overrule her common sense.

She said fretfully, "Does this path go anywhere? Perhaps we should turn back?"

"I believe it's making a gradual circle," he answered, sounding as nonchalant as though they were in the hallway in his own home. "Aren't you enjoying the gardens?"

"It's surely natural that I should be concerned about my sister," she responded stiffly.

"Nonsense." He sounded amused. "She is simply taking a romantic walk, which, after all, is what the place is designed for. Do relax."

Emma felt unable to take his advice. The night was exceptionally dark, and the stars were flung across the sky like silver spangles in a canopy of black velvet. The air had a sweet, intoxicating smell from the flowering shrubs and was, now that they were away from the river, pleasantly warm. The only sound was the soft crunch the earl's boots made on the path. They seemed to be the only people for miles around.

Emma's skin had begun to prickle, as though it had suddenly become extraordinarily sensitive, and she was excruciatingly aware of his fingers on her arm, and of her cloak brushing against his legs.

In a determined effort to reduce the stroll to the commonplace, she rushed into conversation. "In answer to your question about Vauxhall, I find it pleasant enough."

"Such enthusiasm!" he gently mocked.

She shrugged, aware he would feel the gesture. "It seems very contrived to me, a made-up wilderness for city dwellers. I'm not fond of such follies." She gestured toward a miniature Grecian temple that the path was just then circling. "In the country one can have a much greater feeling of freedom and forget man's interfering hand! I enjoyed the boat ride very much, however. I would like to embark on one of those ships, perhaps for Greece or Italy.''

"Ah, so you're a romantic, after all. I had begun to wonder."

"Am I a romantic just because I want new experiences? It's not a quality that greatly appeals to me. I should prefer to be admired for my common sense."

"Now you sound pompous," he remarked, a hint of laughter in his voice.

Emma could feel herself bristle and reflected on how easily he provoked such a reaction in her. It was this edge of annoyance that gave her the courage to ask abruptly, "Why *did* you arrange this outing, my lord? It's scarcely your style. I've felt like a puppet all evening, being moved about to suit your fancy, whatever that is!''

"I think you know why, Emma," he said.

His insinuating tone had the effect of further annoying Emma and of making her wish to lash out at him. She snapped, "I don't recall giving you permission to use my given name!''

"Miss Denton," he substituted agreeably, taking the wind out of her sails.

After a moment she went on crossly, "And I *don't* know why. I can't understand why you're choosing to be mysterious.''

"Or I why you're being obtuse," he said, suddenly sounding frustrated, irritated at her inability to read his mind. "I invited you because it seemed the only way to get you away by yourself. You have a damnable habit of clinging to proprieties!''

"And you of ignoring them!''

"Perhaps... when I want something. And I want you." His fingers bit into the soft skin of her upper arm as he abruptly stopped walking and pulled her to face him.

Emma gasped at the strength of his grip as well as at his blunt words. "I'm not some bit of muslin here for your pleasure!" she said angrily. "You insult me!"

"You call it an insult?" he said softly. "That I think you're beautiful and want to touch your velvety skin? That I imagine your hair loose, flowing around your bare shoulders, my face buried in it?" He lifted one hand and his fingers brushed Emma's temple, then slid into her hair. "That I dream of your lips against mine?"

Somewhere deep inside, Emma was as scandalized by the earl's words and familiar touch as her upbringing had taught her to be, but although she acknowledged that stern voice, it seemed to have lost control. In a daze she felt his fingertips touch the hollow at the base of her throat where her pulse beat. Then his fingers encircled her throat, slid up the slender column of her neck to clasp her chin and tilt her face upward. In the shadowy light from a nearby lamp she could see the wry, tender twist to his mouth, the gleam in his blue eyes. Emma couldn't have moved to save her life; she felt as though her blood had been turned to a thick, hot syrup that flowed sluggishly through her veins, weakening her limbs. Her heart was pounding with hard, quick strokes, which surely he could feel, and her breath was shallow and fast. The quiver in her stomach might have been excitement or fear, she couldn't tell which.

Although she had never before been kissed by a man, it seemed inevitable when his head bent, so slowly that she knew with some part of her mind that he was giving her time to withdraw. Then his lips touched hers. Emma's eyes closed, blinding her to the surroundings, to all else but the surprising warmth and softness of his mouth, which teased and coaxed her own.

The betraying tide of passion crept up on Emma; if it had suddenly swept over her, its newness would have frightened her. Instead, her lips parted tentatively beneath his, and her body swayed toward him, as though seeking his strength.

In an instant the embrace changed. As Ware felt Emma's response, his mouth hardened, forcing open her lips, betraying his sense of urgency. His arms roughly encircled her, crushing her velvet cloak, pressing her slim body against his powerful length. Through the thin muslin of her gown she could feel his heart pounding against her breasts, his strong thighs so shockingly, intimately, touching her own. She might have protested, but her thoughts were too incoherent, the flood of excitement that filled her too intense, so that it seemed more right, more natural, than she had dreamed a man's embrace could be.

And then, through her fog, she heard a sound behind her, and felt him stiffen at the same moment. Footsteps, a light, giggly voice, the rumble of a masculine reply. Emma wrenched herself from the earl's embrace, and a sob escaped her lips. His hand on her arm steadied her, so that she managed to nod with outward composure at the approaching couple who gave them curious looks and a courteous greeting, then passed on.

The instant they were out of sight Ware said, "Emma..." His voice had a thick, uneven timbre, an uncertainty that Emma would have sworn was foreign to the Earl of Ware. "I didn't intend..."

She waited for no more. Her own voice was shaking as she said, "I pray you didn't! If my brother had chanced to be here, he would have to call you out! I said your words were an insult, but for you to have... have mauled me so...!" She whirled and stalked away, stumbling on the dark path because of her unwary pace.

She had no sooner regained her balance than he was beside her, hand gripping her arm. He made no effort to restrain her pace, but simply stayed at her side. Knowing she needed his guidance, knowing that no matter how dangerous his touch, it was more dangerous still for a woman to wander alone at Vauxhall, easy prey for prowling men, she made no effort to shake off his hand.

The truth was that Emma was filled with sick disgust, not aimed at Ware, but herself. She felt her conduct to be inexcusable; either she had committed the unforgivable sin of allowing herself to pitch headlong in love with the Earl of Ware, a man who would never return such love, or else she had been deporting herself like a tavern wench in a haystack, indulging an animal lust with no sense of shame. She had somewhere inside known from the beginning that the earl desired her. It was there to be read in his eyes. She had been equally certain that she had not touched his heart, and yet she had allowed herself to be lured to this lonely path on a dark night, and let him kiss her. She could not even excuse herself by pretending that he had forced her in any way; she had cooperated willingly. Worse yet, she had enjoyed herself!

She suddenly wondered whether he would make an offer for her. Many men, in such a situation, would. She could only pray that his sense of honor was not so strong. What could be more repugnant to her than to have this man, into whose arms she had melted, ask for her hand in marriage out of a feeling of obligation!

What a contrast it would be if he offered for her out of love! That hot light, which she had been barely able to discern in the darkness, would be in his eyes, and his expression would not be mocking, but vulnerable, open to hurt from her, and no other. She rejoiced at the thought, and then knew, with the sharpness of a revelation, that she would accept an offer from him, if only he loved her.

She stumbled again on the path, and his fingers tightened protectively, helping her find her balance. Emma was stunned at the direction her thoughts had taken. Did all of this mean that she was in love with the Earl of Ware? With that dictatorial, mocking, impossible man? The warmth that flooded her face, the speeding of her heartbeat, the extraordinary sensitivity to his presence, even here in the darkness, all told her she had known the answer even before she asked the question. It was because her heart was already given that her body had been so prepared to respond to his. She could scarcely believe she had been able to delude herself for so long into believing she disliked him. He too obviously had all the qualities she had once dreamed of finding in a man; even Godmother would have approved of him.

She was brought out of these absorbing thoughts when Ware abruptly stopped walking and turned her to face him, as though in a replay of his earlier actions. Emma instinctively flinched away and tried to pull free from his grasp. His hand instantly dropped to his side and he stepped back. They stared at each other in tense silence.

Finally he said dryly, "I have no immediate plans to attack you! I simply thought, since we'll be back in the lighted area any moment, and will doubtless find your aunt and uncle there, that you might care to have a moment to compose yourself." He spoke with exaggerated courtesy.

Emma said combatively, "Why should I need to compose myself?"

He suddenly sounded amused. "Because you look as though you have been thoroughly kissed."

Being the object of his amusement succeeded in making her very angry, and she said, in an icy tone, "'Attacked,' I believe, was your word, and considerably more accurate!"

"Be honest, Emma!" he said smugly. "You wanted me to kiss you as much as I wanted to do it. Although I must confess it went further than I intended. Feeling you respond so delightfully went to my head."

Emma gasped. "You...you boor!" She just wished she weren't a lady, and were free to use a stronger term. She could think of several that her brother had carelessly spoken in her presence that could have been applied most accurately to the earl. She went on sharply, "What you, in your lofty arrogance, like to imagine was some favorable response was, instead, shock that someone I had believed to be a gentleman would so forget himself as to handle me in such a way!" She kept her voice low only with an effort. "I defy you to name me an instance when I have displayed any partiality for you. I don't like to be discourteous to any friend of Uncle Max's, but you leave me no choice. I despise you!''

It seemed to her that he recoiled slightly at her words. She had said more than she intended, although not more, she thought, than was justified by his outrageous behavior. The kiss itself had been bad enough, but for him to show no remorse, make no effort to apologize, was almost worse. She could have been coolly forgiving if he had humbled himself as any well-mannered gentleman should have done.

She was more incensed than ever when he took a quick step forward and almost grasped her arm. ''Try to deceive me, if you must,'' he said with sudden intensity, all the laughter gone from his countenance. ''But don't play games with yourself. This is too important! You might fool some callow youngster into thinking he had been mistaken, but I have enough experience to know when a woman trembles in my arms and her lips part sweetly under mine.''

This was the final outrage. Tears of rage sprang into Emma's eyes, and she lifted her hand and swung it at his face, longing to hurt him, if only superficially. She wasn't even allowed this momentary gratification, as his hand intercepted hers before it could strike his cheek.

''Don't you think it might cause talk,'' he said coolly, sounding as though he were remarking on the weather, ''if I have the mark of your fingers on my face? Come, we've absented ourselves long enough. I have no doubt the wandering lambs have long since allowed themselves to be rounded up. I wouldn't want to cause concern for your well-being.''

''No,'' she agreed nastily. ''Then you might have to pay some consequences for your actions!''

He startled her by laughing. "That sounds like my Emma! What consequence is it that you wish I would pay? Would you prefer me to present myself to your uncle, hat in hand, and announce myself ready to kiss the toes of your slippers? Or would you like to see me swing from the gibbet?"

"The second suggestion sounds a good deal more satisfying," she retorted. "And I'm not *your* Emma!"

Again that rich, husky chuckle was her answer. "I like a woman with a sharp tongue," he approved. "Especially," he added, in a caressing voice, "when she possesses other attributes as well."

Frustrated as she was at her inability to best him, the banter had somewhat exhilarated Emma and had had the effect of restoring her customary poise. She reached up to smooth her hair, recalling the way his fingers had twined through it, and discovered that it was falling on her shoulders. Several pins hung askew, and her exploring touch told her that several more doubtless littered the pathway. She struggled to hold the Grecian knot on the back of her head taut while stabbing at it with the pins, which persisted in promptly slithering back out. It was not the first time Emma had had cause to curse her heavy hair.

After watching this unsuccessful battle for a moment, Ware said, "If you'll cry truce, Emma, and let me do that, we might make some progress. I haven't any desire to stand here all night. I think I might make a reasonable lady's maid."

Emma hesitated, then finally, with great reluctance, handed him the pins and turned her back. Common sense was clearly on his side, and she was becoming anxious about the length of time that had passed since they had become separated from the rest of the party.

Immediately Emma felt the gentle, impersonal touch of the earl's fingers in her hair, as he deftly wound the strands into a semblance of their former order and inserted the pins. Emma stayed very still, with bowed head, and tried to ignore the gooseflesh that prickled her spine.

When he had finished, she turned around, saying tartly, "That was remarkably well done. I don't doubt your experience."

"I make no secret of that," he reminded her. "Would you prefer a fumbling schoolboy?"

"I would prefer neither," she snapped. "Your conversation is offensive!"

"Just so you don't say my kisses are," he said softly, then went on before she could find words for her renewed outrage. "Let's put our quarrel aside until another day, Miss Denton." In a curiously formal gesture, considering what had passed between them, he offered her his arm.

Emma was somewhat touched by his effort at conciliation, represented by his reversion to the more proper form of address. She doubted the sincerity of it, but it suited her purposes as well as his to present an unruffled front to her aunt and uncle. Unless she was going to make hysterical accusations about Lord Ware's conduct to her uncle, which she had no intention of doing, it would be best if she gave no one any reason to suspect that they had done more than stroll about in casual search of her sister.

As the earl had predicted, they almost immediately emerged onto a wider path, more populated, then minutes later found themselves on the crowded promenade. Emma realized that the concert was still in progress, although the musicians had switched to a somewhat gayer tune now. She quickly spotted their party and was relieved to see Julia and John Hartley under their mother's wing. She could see, even from a distance, that Aunt Helen appeared agitated, and guiltily attributed it to her own disappearance.

The moment they reached the others, Mrs. Barlow cried, "Emma! Thank the Lord! We've been so worried! I don't know what to do! Your uncle and the others are searching, but what can so few hope to accomplish?"

Emma suddenly realized that her mouth was hanging unattractively open, and snapped it shut. "Aunt, what are you talking about? You can see that I'm safe. Surely we can find Uncle Max..." She stopped and looked around. "Where's Georgiana?" she asked, an uneasy feeling taking grip.

"She's disappeared!" Mrs. Barlow declared dramatically. "I'm beginning to fear she's been kidnapped, or... It could be anything!"

Lady Hartley explained more calmly, "We felt certain you were safe with the earl, and we hoped that somehow you had met Georgiana and were merely taking a roundabout way back. But obviously you didn't encounter her?" The last was a question.

Dumbly Emma shook her head. If the wanderer had been Julia, Emma would not have been overly concerned; Julia would doubtless have considered being "lost" at Vauxhall a delicious lark. She stood now at her mother's side, her dark eyes eager and a tiny hint of a smile tugging at her mouth, as though she were greatly enjoying the furor. Such behavior, however, was foreign to Georgiana, who would be frightened without a strong arm to lend her support, and who in any case had too much sensitivity to wish to cause her relatives anxiety.

It was the earl who said, in a commonsensical way, "Perhaps, Mr. Hartley, you could tell us how you came to lose Miss Georgiana. You were certainly together when we last saw you."

The young man flushed under Ware's critical gaze. "I don't know," he said wretchedly. "It sounds absurd, but...one moment she was with me, and the next she was gone. She pointed out a flower in bloom to one side of the path, so I turned to look, and when I turned back she had disappeared. I called for her, and there was no answer. Surely if she had been dragged away there would have been even a little bit of a scuffle, some hint of distress...!"

"Were there intersecting paths there?"

He nodded. "She could have gone in any direction, even back the way we had come. I thought she might have become distressed that her aunt was not in sight, and turned back in search of her, not realizing I was not following, and become confused in the dark. I can think of no other explanation!"

Ware remarked, "It sounds very much as though Miss Georgiana gave you the slip deliberately. And if that's the case, she'll turn up when it suits her. I suggest, however, that somebody stay here, should she come looking, and the rest of us split up in pairs and commence a search. Vauxhall is not so large that she can stay hidden for long!"

In the end Lady Hartley and Julia stayed where they were, to be on the lookout for Georgiana, should she appear in the crowd, while Emma and the earl took one path and John Hartley and Mrs. Barlow another.

Ware thought it best for Aunt Helen and Emma, the two who had the most cause for fear, to take action and not be left standing to brood.

Emma gave only a passing thought to the fact that she was once again alone in the darkness with the earl, but her increasing fear for her sister's safety preoccupied her to the exclusion of all else. This was no leisurely stroll, either. Ware set a brisk pace, pausing only to peer around bushes at the occasional bench, which had been placed to ensure privacy. Under normal circumstances Emma would have been amused by the expressions on the faces of one couple who were cuddled together, taking full advantage of the privacy. They were clearly shocked by the intrusion, and appeared only a little mollified by the earl's muttered, "Damn! I beg your pardon!"

Emma couldn't imagine what he expected to find, as it seemed unlikely in the extreme to her that her sister would be sitting on a bench alone in the dark, or be sharing it with a stranger. It seemed best, however, not to pass up any possibility, however remote, so she made no comment on these detours.

In the agreed-upon time, having found no sign of Georgiana, they returned to the promenade, there to find the other searchers, including Uncle Max, before them. Charles and Lydia, who stood close together, had apparently had their walk alone after all, but unfortunately not the romantic one her brother might have wished for.

Uncle Max, although looking haggard, turned to Emma and Ware, saying in his calm way, "I'm beginning to be alarmed. I thought it most likely she had simply wandered off by accident, and has been slow in making her way back, but so much time has passed now that I fear some misadventure must have befallen her. Perhaps we should ask the assistance of the authorities.''

He had no sooner finished speaking when the earl said, ''That won't be necessary. Here comes Miss Georgiana now, and looking none the worse for her adventure.''

As one they turned to see Georgiana hurrying toward them. Her hair seemed to be in some disarray, but otherwise, as the earl had noted, she appeared much as usual.

Her soft cheeks were touched with pink as she stopped, saying in a breathless way, ''I'm so sorry! Did I worry you? I don't know how I came to be separated from Mr. Hartley, and then I got so muddled...'' She made a helpless gesture with one hand. ''Emma, you know how bad my sense of direction has always been! And it's so dark! I'm sorry!'' she repeated, her curiously bright gaze flicking from one face to another.

Emma couldn't help wondering why Georgiana had hurried in such a way to explain, instead of giving vent to the relief she must surely be feeling at being reunited with her family. It was as though she had memorized her excuses, and needed to say them quickly, before she forgot her story.

Emma chided herself for thinking such a thing about her sister, who was surely incapable of deceit, but then, almost unbelievingly, she saw the tiny, conspiratorial smile Georgiana gave Julia, so quick that it could almost have been imagined. Emma's eyes met Ware's and she saw that he, too, had seen. His face remained carefully expressionless, but there was no doubt that he had understood, just as she had, that this entire escapade had been planned by the two girls, to what purpose Emma couldn't guess, although that smile seemed to imply that it had been a success.

Apparently no one else had observed the interchange, because the others were chattering away in their relief and making much of poor Georgiana, who must have been so frightened alone, and had managed so well. Only Lydia appeared faintly disapproving of the younger girl's carelessness. Julia and Georgiana very deliberately did not look at each other again, and Georgiana fell so well into her role that Emma could almost persuade herself her suspicions were groundless. Another glance at Ware, who stood back a little from the others, served to convince her to the contrary, however, and she determined to have the truth from her sister the moment she could get her alone.

They chose not to stay to see the fireworks, which in any case had been delayed for some reason. The crowd was growing restive, as this was the main attraction for many. The spirit had gone out of the occasion for their party; Aunt Helen declared that her heart was still fluttering, and Lady Hartley was keeping a tight grip on Julia's arm. John Hartley was sulking, and Emma gathered that he had come to the same conclusion as had the earl, that Georgiana had deliberately left him. Charles, whose emotions and concerns seldom ran deep, was the only one, with the possible exception of Julia, disappointed at the decision to forgo the fireworks.

The earl had felt that the river crossing would lose its attraction late in the evening, when everybody was tired, so he had planned their return journey by road. The carriages were waiting outside the entrance, and in a very few minutes Emma prepared to follow her aunt and uncle and sister up the carriage steps.

Ware, who stood beside the open door, said courteously, "Thank you for your company, Miss Denton." His smile, however, put another connotation altogether on his words.

Emma nodded curtly and made to pass him. Just as she bent her head to enter the carriage, she heard him say softly, "Another time, Miss Denton," and felt it to be a threat.

She could only look on the evening as an ordeal that had thankfully passed. She was left with several tasks, the most important of which was to put the Earl of Ware out of her mind and forget that her heart—not to mention her body—had ever weakened toward him. She also needed to find out what her sister had been up to. She prayed that it had been some innocent, girlish scheme, dreamed up by Julia, and that there were no serious ramifications.

CHAPTER SEVEN

THE FOLLOWING DAY began with two confrontations, both of an uncomfortable nature. The first was with Georgiana, and was of Emma's doing. Emma didn't believe in putting off distasteful duties.

Georgiana, like Charles (and Papa, of course), was not an early riser. On a usual morning she sipped her chocolate in bed at about ten-thirty, and it was at this unguarded hour that Emma chose to speak with her.

Georgiana was indeed propped against her pillows with a mug of steaming hot chocolate on a tray balanced on the coverlet. She started when she saw Emma, who fancied that her sister was not altogether pleased to see her. Then Georgiana's pretty face cleared, and she said in a soft, breathless voice, "Oh, Emma, am I late?" She struggled upright. "I'll be down directly if you'll call Jane. Isn't Lady Bidwell's garden party this afternoon? The roses should be so lovely!"

Emma advanced on the bed. "No, no, you needn't hurry." She adroitly cut off her sister's escape route by sitting on the side of the bed. "The garden party *is* this afternoon, but we won't be leaving for several hours. I wanted to talk to you privately."

Although there was no discernible change in her sister's expression, Emma sensed Georgiana's tension. One tiny hand clutched at the ruffles at her slender throat, as though protectively, and her lovely blue eyes widened with frightened innocence. "You sound so very stern, Emma! Is something wrong?"

Emma hesitated. How did one accuse one's sister of being a liar and a schemer? She should have better thought out her plan beforehand.

At length she approached the matter indirectly. "We were very worried about you last night, Georgiana. Vauxhall is a dangerous place for a young girl to wander alone."

Georgiana's rosebud mouth opened impulsively, then closed. After a moment she said with obvious restraint, "I *am* sorry if I frightened you, Emma. It seemed safe to walk with Mr. Hartley. I know you approve of him."

Emma refused to be diverted. "Walking with Mr. Hartley *would* have been safe."

Her sister gave an unconvincing laugh. "It was foolish of me to become lost, wasn't it? Charles said I was shatter-brained! But since no harm came of it . . . I won't do such a thing again, Emma. I promise to be more careful."

More careful in what way? Emma wondered. About being discovered? Georgiana was not a good dissembler. She sounded genuinely sorry to have worried her family, but her story of how it came about didn't ring true.

Emma said bluntly, "Georgiana, you can't hoax me. I've known you far too long. And why should you wish to? Surely I'm not such a martinet that you need be afraid to tell me anything. Nor am I such a fool that I don't know you and Julia arranged last night's escapade. Tell me why, and I promise not to involve Aunt Helen or Uncle Max."

The younger girl stole a quick glance at her sister. "I can't tell you, Emma," she said in a low voice. "I won't tell you. Don't ask me."

Emma's mouth nearly dropped open. She stared at the top of her sister's bowed head. "Georgiana," she began quietly, and with commendable restraint, "since Mama died I've tried to be a sort of mother to you. And I hoped we were friends."

"Emma, I want to tell you, but you'd never understand!" Georgiana said, her voice rising to a wail. "Can't you trust me?"

"Should I?"

There was no answer. Emma went on, as patiently as she knew how, "You are far too young to make sensible decisions. And you've been so protected. It would be easy for someone to take advantage of your soft heart. And, don't you see, we have trusted you! Perhaps too much!"

At that Georgiana spoke with sudden defiance. "It was just in fun! Perhaps it *was* silly, but you're not my mother, you're only my sister, and you don't have any right to treat me like...like some dog that misbehaved! I'm a person, too, you know, and I don't need to always be managed, even if you and Charles *do* think I'm a sapskull!"

Emma frowned a little and protested, "I am certain *I* have never said such a thing!" Guiltily she reflected that it would have been better if she could also have asserted with equal vehemence that she had never even thought such a thing. "And Charles," she went on, "says a great deal he doesn't mean, as you should know." She sighed, sensing that whatever advantage she had possessed was gone. Georgiana was entrenched in a mood of righteous anger now and was unlikely to retreat. Her attack had been so pointed that Emma had to take care not to feel or sound defensive about what was, after all, justifiable concern.

On that thought she stood up, merely adding, "I sympathize with your desire to try your wings. Nonetheless, London is a far different and more dangerous place than Yorkshire, and you are too young and untried to be allowed your freedom, whether you would have it so or not! And foolish as the proprieties often seem to me, you and I *must* conform to them if we are to take our places as members of the ton and succeed in making respectable marriages. Do you understand?"

When no reply was forthcoming, Emma hardened her voice and said, "Let me warn you, Georgiana. If you further jeopardize your respectability, we will consider the season at an end and post home with no further ado. Is that clear?"

The mulish look was now more pronounced. "You needn't be so dramatic! I promised to be more careful, didn't I? You won't have any cause for complaint!" Her chin was set at a proud angle.

Emma regarded her in silence for a moment, then said quietly, "I accept your reassurance, Georgy. Just remember not to attempt to feed me any more Banbury tales! And..." She hesitated. "You *can* trust me, you know. I want for you only what will make you happiest."

Her sister made no answer, so Emma left the room, trying to ignore the bleak chasm that seemed to have opened in her stomach. She was surprised to find that she cared so much about her relationship with Georgiana. She had always believed herself a good sister to the young girl, but now it was obvious her belief had been a delusion.

Emma wondered why she was so certain she was not overreacting to the previous night's incident. To all appearances it had been no more than a girlish lark, the sort of nonsense Julia Hartley might have dreamed up as a daring escapade. And yet that didn't sound like Georgiana, who was afraid of the shadows in her own bedroom. Surely strong motivation would have been required to induce her to set off alone in the dark pathways at Vauxhall!

Could her sister have slipped away to meet some lover whom she knew her family would consider unacceptable? Emma wondered. This solution to the mystery would have been more appealing if Georgiana had displayed any indication of developing a *tendre* for one of her many suitors, but, Sir James Finkirk aside, there had been no such indication. They had not encountered Sir James for weeks, and therefore Georgiana had had no opportunity to make an assignation with the man, even assuming she would have consented to do so.

Here Emma had to give a disbelieving shake of her head. That she could even be considering whether Georgiana would have taken such a course was evidence of how seriously damaged her relationship with her sister was, and how little she really knew her. Perhaps she had made a mistake in bringing Georgiana to London for the season. Her sister might have been happier if she had been allowed to marry a modest country squire and take her place in the milieu in which she was at home.

Just then Emma became conscious of a discreet throat clearing, and turned about to face the butler. "Yes, Tompkins?"

"Mr. Linley has called, Miss Denton. I've shown him into the blue drawing room."

"Oh, dear," Emma exclaimed involuntarily. Hastily calling her tongue to order, she added, "I'll be right down. Thank you."

She proceeded to her room, where she quickly changed to a less serviceable gown and smoothed her hair before hastening down the stairs to the drawing room. When she appeared in the doorway, Mr. Linley rose to his feet and came toward her, one hand outstretched.

"You're a ray of sunshine this morning," he complimented, somewhat tritely, Emma thought, referring to her daffodil-yellow muslin gown.

Emma hid her dismay and answered with composure, "Thank you. I could wish the day had been endowed with more sunshine instead. We had planned to attend Lady Bidwell's garden fete this afternoon, but I fear it looks like rain. Shall we see you there, weather permitting?"

"Yes...no...I received an invitation, but..." He broke off this confusing train of words and said instead, a question in his voice, "Emma?"

Emma reached for the bellrope and said brightly, "May I offer you some refreshment?"

He had not moved. "Thank you, but no. Emma, surely you can guess what I've come to speak to you about."

Of course she had guessed. She had not missed the reproachful looks Mr. Linley had cast at her the evening before, when she had reappeared in the earl's company. The moment Tompkins had announced that Mr. Linley had called at such an unfashionably early hour, Emma had known his purpose, which had no doubt been advanced by last evening's events.

She tried to let none of her thoughts show on her face as she seated herself on the satinwood sofa and looked up to meet Mr. Linley's imploring gaze.

"Yes, I think I can guess," she said quietly. "But . . . I don't know what I should say . . ."

"Let me speak first." He stepped forward eagerly and took Emma's soft hand in his own. "Emma, you must have guessed how I've come to feel about you."

She wished he would cease assuming she had read his mind. It was ungentlemanlike for him to imply that she spent all her time speculating on how he felt for her. She said nothing, waiting for him to go on.

"I think the moment I met you I knew you were the woman I wanted to be my wife and the mother of my sons," he said with dignity. "You are lovely, and yet have such grace, such . . . such restraint. It is impossible to imagine you indulging in unbecoming conduct. You are so different from the other young girls, who seem to have nothing in their heads but fluff!"

Emma wished she could believe he was complimenting her on her intellect, but she feared this was not the case. It did not seem to her that Mr. Linley would welcome great intellectual attainments in his wife. Instead, it appeared he wanted a woman whom he could present to his neighbors with pride, who would never be flustered or show great emotions, who would never indulge in any absurdities, who would, in short, always appear to be above the fray. She wondered what he expected of this model of decorum at night, alone in their bedchamber. He *had* said the mother of his sons, so presumably he did expect to beget some.

Emma was aware that Mr. Linley's lips were still moving, but his words failed to penetrate. Her mind kept turning back to the image of herself lying beside him in the warm cocoon of a canopied bed. Would she feel as she had when Ware's arms were about her, and his strong thighs pressed against hers? Would she feel abandoned and wanton, tender and sweet and wild? And if she felt so, would Mr. Linley welcome the flowering of these emotions, or would he expect his wife to accept his lovemaking in a dignified, dutiful manner, displaying great restraint?

Emma wondered whether his touch would indeed ignite such feelings. Perhaps she was a trollop, with overheated emotions, and had responded to Ware merely because he was a man, and the night had been dark and close. She looked up at Linley's straight, firm lips, and said, "Would you care to kiss me?"

She realized that he had been talking and that she had interrupted him. He looked both astonished and unsure. Her invitation, however, was one he could scarcely ignore.

She had anticipated that he would sweep her to her feet and into his arms, pulling her body against his, but instead, he hesitated for an instant, then sat carefully beside her on the sofa. Still holding her hand in his, he leaned forward and decorously pressed his lips against hers. They were warm and dry and firm against her own, which were being squished against her teeth. She was uncertain how to respond. How did one kiss a man back? Before she could react, however, Mr. Linley's lips left hers, and he was once more sitting upright, looking expectantly at her.

Did he consider the kiss a seal of their engagement? she wondered. Or was he merely waiting for Emma's answer?

"I'm sorry," she heard herself say.

"Sorry for what?" He laughed a little nervously. "I think, under these circumstances, that even your aunt couldn't consider a kiss improper."

With great effort Emma pulled her scattered thoughts into some kind of order. She had been drilled in what to say when a gentleman made her an offer, so as not to appear too eager, or, should she be refusing, not to carelessly slight his consequence.

"I'm more honored than I can say by your offer," she began formally. "But I'm afraid I can't marry you, and I'm very sorry. You're everything I've always thought I sought in a husband, and I suspect I may be sorry I refused you, but..." She hesitated, her sympathetic gaze holding his. "I hold you in great esteem, but I don't love you, and I've come to realize how important that is. It wouldn't be right for me to accept your offer."

She could detect only bewilderment in his eyes. He stammered, "But...why did you ask me to kiss you?"

"It was very wrong of me," she said. She found herself blushing, and for the first time in their conversation evaded his gaze. She couldn't tell him the truth, which was that she had wished to compare his kiss with the earl's and therefore discover how strong were her feelings for Ware. She had needed to know whether she could make herself feel such passion for another man, one far more suitable as a husband. "It helped me be certain," she said. "I *wanted* to feel more for you."

Resentment had begun to cloud his face, and he drew back from her a little, his nostrils flaring. "As one would try out a horse's paces?" he asked cuttingly.

His accusation was too near the mark, and Emma bit her lower lip. "I'm sorry if you should think it so. I could wish we might part without anger, although perhaps that, too, is cowardly of me."

Her plea failed in its purpose, apparently going unheard. "It's Ware, isn't it?" he demanded.

"No gentleman would expect a lady to answer that question," Emma returned evenly.

"If you expect to catch Ware—" he began hotly, but was interrupted by a light tap on the door, which then swung open. Tompkins, expressionless as always, stood in the doorway. "The Earl of Ware, Miss Denton."

Emma glanced desperately from Mr. Linley's angry, but now composed, face to the butler's. Her visitors could not be allowed to meet, not when Mr. Linley was in his present state of mind. He might well say something unforgivable to the earl.

"Mr. Linley was just leaving," she said as calmly as she was able. "Please show him out." As her gaze met the butler's, she saw that he understood very well, and concluded that he had been listening at the keyhole, or at least hovering very close to the door. At any other time Emma would have been angry, but now she was relieved. It was clear to her that Tompkins had determined that Emma required assistance and had deliberately interrupted the unpleasant interchange.

"Certainly, miss." He inclined his head slightly and stepped aside, waiting for Mr. Linley to precede him out the door. The butler somehow succeeded in appearing both deferential and commanding at the same time.

Mr. Linley hesitated for an instant, clearly annoyed by the dismissal, but good manners triumphed and he gave a stiff bow, without taking Emma's hand in his, and muttered, "Good day. Please give my regards to your aunt."

Emma politely murmured, "Indeed I will," and watched with relief as he turned toward the door.

Her relief, however, was premature. Before Mr. Linley could exit the room, his way was blocked by the Earl of Ware, who with raised brows and every indication of interest surveyed Linley's usually pleasant face, now set in rigid lines.

He finally smiled. "I'm surprised to see you out so early, Linley. I didn't think you shared Miss Denton's and my proclivity for, ah—" here he shot a swift glance of amusement at Emma "—early-morning activities."

Emma glowered at the earl, who had clearly made this remark only to provoke poor Mr. Linley. It achieved its intent, as Linley's hands balled into fists and his face became suffused with blood, giving him the look of one of the helpless, enraged animals at a bearbaiting contest.

Emma said sharply, "I hardly think our *one* morning ride gives us a great deal in common, my lord. Mr. Linley, I'm sure Aunt Helen will be sorry she missed you." Since Aunt Helen was doubtless ensconced in the breakfast room, comfortably lingering over her morning chocolate, this was a piece of sophistry, but it served its purpose.

Mr. Linley gave Emma one last baffled look, nodded abruptly, then blundered from the room, followed by Tompkins, who had stared woodenly ahead throughout this exchange, giving no evidence of hearing a single word. The door closed behind the butler with a tiny click, and Emma wondered at his willingness to leave her alone with a succession of gentlemen. Had Aunt Helen given specific instructions in the expectation that certain of Emma's suitors would seek privacy to make offers?

Ware strolled toward Emma, still with that unpleasantly knowing smile quirking his lips. "Sent him about his business, did you?" he observed, and although it was ostensibly a question, Emma doubted that he required or expected an answer.

She responded tartly, "Do you often wander about other people's homes, entering any room you choose without waiting to be announced? You must overhear many interesting conversations!"

He appeared untouched by her acerbity. "I was curious," he said mildly. "Old Stone Face—" he jerked his head toward the door "—actually looked agitated. I thought perhaps a gallant knight was required to rush to the rescue."

"Nonsense!"

"What? You doubt my sincerity?" He grinned. "Actually, I recognized Linley's pretty pair standing out front and guessed why he was here. He was far from happy last night, you know."

Emma had no intention of amiably discussing the other man. She retorted, "He would have been even less happy if he could have guessed how outrageously you behaved."

She was immediately sorry she had raised the matter, because her words effected a transformation in the earl. He gave a slow, appreciative smile, and his dark blue eyes seemed to glow as he let his gaze move from Emma's flushed cheeks down over her slim body and back up, lingering on the white skin exposed just above the low, ruffled neckline of her gown. Her heart began to beat so fast she felt breathless, and she had to suppress an urgent desire to cross her arms protectively over her chest.

Ware finally said, on a note of laughter, "It is not my behavior your Mr. Linley would find objectionable, but yours. No man would like to see the woman with whom he imagines himself in love passionately returning another man's kiss."

Emma made an inarticulate protest and turned away, clenching her fists at her physical response to this uncaring creature. Why, instead, could not her heart have pounded and her knees weakened for Mr. Linley?

The earl asked abruptly, "Did you kiss him?"

Emma swung back to face him and said defiantly, "Yes!"

All trace of humor was gone from his face. For a long, silent moment tension leaped between them as his narrowed blue eyes held Emma's mutinous gray-green ones. Then he gave a contemptuous shrug and said dismissively, "Linley wouldn't dare forget you're a lady long enough to hold you like a woman! It wouldn't suit his notions of what's proper."

Emma gave a tiny smile, feigning amusement, and said coolly, "He didn't act as though he felt too constrained. Personally, I find one kiss to be rather like another."

Ware gave a growl in the back of his throat, and his long, brown fingers closed painfully on Emma's slender shoulders. "You lie!" he said harshly. "Your lips parted for mine like a flower for the sun! You're too innocent to find such pleasure in just any man's touch! You want me, just as I want you!" He gave her a little shake.

Emma jerked back from his grasp, nearly hissing like a cat in her fury and the ache in her injured shoulder. "Don't speak to me of wanting! I'm neither for sale nor for hire, like your customary wants! Satisfy your... your lust elsewhere, and leave me alone!"

"Emma..." He reached for her again, although this time his voice had a different note in it, one Emma was too angry to define. To her enormous relief, he had no time to continue, because just then the door opened and Aunt Helen came bubbling into the room, looking expectantly from one to the other. The earl's hand fell back to his side, and he turned to greet Mrs. Barlow, his face impassive and his emotions already neatly tucked away from sight. Emma, too, took a deep breath and managed a semblance of a smile.

"Good morning, Aunt. The weather doesn't look promising, does it?"

"No, and it's a pity. Lady Bidwell's roses are particularly fine. But who knows? It's not raining yet!" She was studying Emma's face in evident puzzlement.

Ware said then, "I called in hopes Miss Denton would come riding with me. I feel sure the rain will hold off that long. Wouldn't you enjoy some fresh air?"

Because of Mrs. Barlow's presence, Emma had to bite back the scathing opinion of the earl's impudence that had leaped to her lips. She drew in a sharp breath and let her eyes meet his. The grim line of his mouth had softened and one dark brow quirked above the deep blue eyes, which held an apology and even, Emma fancied, a look of pleading. Her fury instantly died.

She suddenly realized how stifling was the air in the drawing room. A fire burned merrily on the grate, more than successfully combating the gray sky outside the windows. She thought longingly how refreshing the damp, cool breeze would be. She could let Caspar gallop, shaking out both her horse's fidgets and her own. It wouldn't be difficult to treat the earl with cool civility, pretending this morning's events had never taken place.

She finally nodded and said temperately, "That would be pleasant. If you wouldn't mind waiting while I change?"

"Not at all."

Aunt Helen didn't hide her satisfaction. "Don't worry about Lady Bidwell's fete, Emma. She'll doubtless have to move it indoors, and think how tedious that will be! To stand about pretending fascination with the conversation of the same dull people one saw just the other night.... If you're not home in time, I may escort Georgiana. I don't care to disappoint her, but your presence isn't required."

"Thank you, Aunt Helen," Emma said calmly. "But I feel sure I'll be home in good time. Now if you'll excuse me?"

Mrs. Barlow scurried after her into the hall. "Emma!" she hissed, glancing back toward the open drawing room door. "What about Mr. Linley? Don't leave me in suspense! Did he..."

Emma said, without hope, "Aunt Helen, couldn't we talk about it another time?" She met her aunt's imploring gaze, then sighed. "Yes, he did," she admitted. "But I said no."

"Because of..." Aunt Helen jerked her head toward the earl's unseen presence.

"No!" Emma exclaimed sharply, then realized she would be wise to lower her voice. "No, I just didn't feel I...I could care for Mr. Linley enough." She hesitated, then asked quietly, "Are you very disappointed?"

Aunt Helen looked astonished. "Disappointed? Oh, no! My hopes for you lie in quite another direction!" She gave another meaningful glance toward the drawing room, smiled beatifically, then turned away, presumably with the intention of entertaining the earl while he waited for Emma.

Emma hurried up the stairs to her room, where she gave vent to her annoyance by a vicious kick at the washstand. Of course this only had the effect of injuring her toes, which angered her still further.

A SHORT TIME LATER she and Ware were clattering through the streets toward Hyde Park. The necessity for controlling their fractious mounts limited the opportunity for conversation, and when they arrived at the park, Emma was pleased to see that it was relatively deserted. Some hardy souls were strolling and a few grooms were exercising horses, but it appeared that the chill day, which held such a threat of rain, had persuaded the majority of people to stay indoors.

Without waiting for the earl to turn in the gate behind her, Emma set her heels to Caspar's side and loosened her reins at the same time. Her chestnut needed no persuading to spring forward in a gallop, his long strides eating up the distance. Emma had no intention of inviting a race, so she was unsurprised when Ware's gray stallion soon caught up, and the two horses cantered side by side as they swung around and started back.

They were on their third circuit, Emma well ahead because Ware had briefly paused to speak to an acquaintance, when, out of the corner of her eye, Emma caught a glimpse of a man standing nearly obscured by some shrubbery. She was briefly irritated, feeling the man should know better. His presence could easily make a high-strung horse bolt.

She had passed him, though, and put him from her mind, when suddenly something slammed into her shoulder from behind, nearly knocking her from the saddle. She thought she heard a crack, as though a branch had broken, but Caspar bolted at the sound and was galloping wildly. Emma was half out of the saddle, clinging to his whipping mane with her right hand, since her entire left arm seemed to have gone numb.

Caspar turned toward some trees and she began to feel inexplicably weak, unable to stop his progress. With a rush of relief she became aware of Thor, edging alongside. Ware's big hand pushed Emma upright in the saddle, then grasped the reins from her hand. He used Thor's powerful body to push Caspar away from the trees, into a wide circle that gradually slowed. When he had finally brought the big chestnut to a halt, he turned to Emma, his eyes blazing.

"What the hell happened?" Abruptly his expression changed, and she saw that he was staring at her left shoulder. She twisted her neck to look down at herself and saw the blood that had soaked the fawn-colored fabric. Still she felt nothing, and she looked up, puzzled, at the earl.

Without hesitation he leaned toward her and pulled back the neck of her gown with one gentle hand to make a quick inspection. Emma made no protest. Finally, in answer to her unspoken question, Ware said baldly, "You've been shot."

"Shot? In Hyde Park?" Insensibly, she began to laugh, then as quickly sobered when she saw the look of intense anger on his face. "Are you sure?" she asked.

"I'm sure," he said tersely. "I was on the Peninsula, you know. I've seen enough men shot." He soothed his restless horse. "Does it hurt?"

She ignored his question. "Aren't you going to try to capture the man?" she demanded. Twisting in her saddle, she pointed with her good arm back toward the cluster of shrubbery where the man had been. "He was there. I noticed him, but . . ." She began to shrug, then thought better of it. Tentatively, she touched her blood-soaked shoulder, wondering why she felt nothing.

For an instant there was a glitter in the earl's eyes, like the light reflecting from the honed edge of a sword blade, then impatience mixed with regret wiped that momentary look of cold determination from his face. "He'll have fled long since," he said. "In any case, you're more important. Now answer my question. Does your shoulder pain you?"

Emma shook her head. "It's hard to move my hand, but I can't feel anything."

"Don't worry," he advised in his usual cool fashion. "That often happens. I've known people to break a leg and not even feel it." He was unwinding the starched white cravat from about his neck. He held Emma's gaze. "Can you control Caspar?" he asked. When she nodded and took the reins from him, he folded the linen into a triangle.

"Are you going to tie that on me?" Emma asked, feeling a surprising detachment.

Ware looked up. "Yes, but only as a sling to hold your arm and shoulder still. You don't seem to be bleeding badly, but I'm afraid the ride home is going to jostle your wound. It will hurt eventually, you know." He hesitated, and she saw the momentary indecision on his face. "I could send for a carriage, of course, but . . . I don't like the idea of delaying. I want the doctor to see you immediately."

Emma felt the first thrill of fear. Ware's air of matter-of-fact competence had kept her from worrying, trivialized the incident. Now she could see that his calmness had been partly a mask, worn for her benefit.

"Am I going to die?" she asked, staring straight into his eyes, watching for the flicker that might give away the truth.

"No!" he exclaimed harshly. "Don't talk like that!" For a second his hand was almost rough as he pushed her arm against her body, then wound the makeshift sling about it and tied it behind her neck. He was so close that she felt as much as heard the deep breath he drew. When he spoke again he was once more in control, his voice soothing and calm. "I believe it to be just a flesh wound. You're bleeding in front, so the bullet must have come out again. You should have no difficulty unless the bullet damaged something, perhaps broke a bone. That's why you need the doctor. Besides, he'll give you something to keep it from hurting.''

''But it doesn't...'' she began to protest, then bit off her words as Caspar shifted under her and she felt the first distant throbbing. It was almost a relief, as she had begun to fear she might never again feel anything in her arm. It was that which had frightened her. She could see that she wasn't bleeding to death; she had lost only enough blood to stain a dark red path on the front and, she presumed, the back of her riding habit. She was glad she had not ruined her Hessian-blue riding dress, she thought irrelevantly; the fawn was not nearly as becoming.

The earl took the leather reins from her hand and turned the horses toward the gate, keeping them to a slow walk. Emma stared numbly between her horse's flickering ears, trying to think of nothing in particular. The throbbing, as impersonal as the first echo of distant thunder, was becoming sharper, tearing at her flesh. When another horse clattered by, startling Caspar into a prance, Emma winced and then gritted her teeth.

Ware shot her a quick look and said, in a rough voice, ''Emma...''

Emma didn't even hear. ''It wasn't an accident!'' she said wonderingly.

''An accident? I should think not! Hyde Park is scarcely the usual place to practice one's aim!''

Emma gave an impatient shake of her head. ''No, no, I didn't mean this. I meant the coach.''

The horses were walking side by side, so Emma found herself staring directly into Ware's blue eyes, which held a mixture of puzzlement and that same ferocious anger she had earlier glimpsed.

"What the devil do you mean?" he nearly snarled.

Emma's head felt light, filled with air, perhaps like one of those absurd hot-air balloons, which seemed to float free from the earth so easily. She shook it, closing her eyes for a moment. "I'm sorry," she mumbled. "I forgot.... I was nearly run down by a coach, right in Berkeley Square, just last week. It looked as though the horses were being driven right at me, but that seemed ridiculous. I have no enemies. So I thought it must be an accident."

"But now you know better," Ware said flatly.

"Yes."

"Emma." He turned his head again to look at her. "Who is it? Who is trying to kill you?"

"I don't know!" Emma cried. "I can't think!"

"No. Of course not. I'm sorry." His big hand came out to grip hers, sending warmth and reassurance through her in a flood. "Don't worry. You'll be safe at home in no time."

Safe? she reflected. She felt safe now, with Ware. If only he had been closer in the park, no one would have dared shoot at her, surely. She saw then that they were turning into the square and nearly giggled. She was beginning to make a habit of returning home in wild disarray. This was the most extreme, of course. How she would frighten everyone!

CHAPTER EIGHT

WITH HER MAID'S ASSISTANCE, Emma eased the pale lime sarcenet gown over the bandage on her shoulder. She tried to suppress her excitement, telling herself it was nonsense; Lord Ware was merely performing the expected courtesy in calling to see her so soon. After all, as her escort he surely felt some sense of responsibility for her mishap.

When she stepped quietly into the salon, Ware was staring out the window at the square, his broad back to her. Taking advantage of his unawareness of her presence, Emma paused for an instant to let her gaze run lovingly over him, from the proud angle of his dark head to his muscular calves, emphasized by gleaming Hessians topped with jaunty tassels.

She bit her lip to stem the flood of weakness that had nearly broken free in her body. After a moment she was able to say calmly, giving nothing of her thoughts away, "It's kind of you to call so soon, my lord."

He spun around, his blue eyes raking her, settling first on the outline of the bandage and then on her still-pale face.

She went on, in the same voice she might have used for any of the dozens of callers who graced the Barlows' drawing room in a given week, "As you can see,

I'm very nearly restored. All I needed was a few days' rest.''

"Should you be up?" the earl asked abruptly. "What did the doctor say?"

Emma's brows rose slightly at his peremptory tone, but she answered, "That it was just a flesh wound, as you guessed. He said the temporary numbness was very common, and nothing to be concerned about. It hurts only a little now, and I won't even need the bandage for long."

Ware continued to look searchingly at her, as though he doubted her word. Did he expect her to slide gracefully into a faint at his feet, as any self-respecting heroine should do? For a moment Emma wished she were less stalwart. Any female with an ounce of romanticism in her soul would begin to sway, press one delicate hand to her brow, let him catch her in his arms...

Suddenly the earl said, in a hard voice, "And now what? You've been lucky twice. What about the next time?"

"Next time?" Emma repeated idiotically. "I have no enemies!"

He made an exasperated sound. "For God's sake, Emma, surely you've been *thinking*! Who could possibly want you dead?"

"Nobody!" she cried. "Nobody! It makes no sense!"

"What about your fortune?" he asked implacably. "Who is your heir?"

"I don't want to talk about it!" Emma was close to screaming. "Don't you understand? I've thought and thought, and it doesn't do any good! The whole thing doesn't make sense, and I don't want to think about it anymore!''

His hand grasped her elbow, preventing her from turning away. She didn't try to pull free, just stood looking up into his eyes. When he spoke again, his voice was gentle. ''Emma, you can't hide from this. What you want, or what I want, means nothing. All that counts is what someone else wants. If you are to be safe, we need to know who that is, and what he wants.''

Emma drew a deep, shuddering breath. ''I appreciate your concern, my lord,'' she said mechanically, ''but it is not your problem, so...''

''Don't be a fool!'' he snapped, his fingers tightening on her bare arm. ''And don't be so damned polite! If you're trying to tell me to leave you alone, say so!''

''Very well.'' Her chin rose and she stepped back from his grasp. ''Leave me alone. Let me handle my own life. And,'' she added illogically, ''don't call me Emma. I don't like it.''

He laughed, and she could sense the tension draining from him. ''That's my Emma.'' He forestalled her reproof. ''I'll strike a bargain with you. I hate being addressed as 'my lord' by you. I do have a name. If you'll call me Richard, I'll use a proper Miss Denton.''

''Don't be ridiculous! What would my uncle say? And you needn't laugh like that! Is this any time for levity?'' She glared at him. ''Now if you're satisfied as to my well-being, why don't you leave?''

The laugh was gone in an instant, leaving his eyes glittering and his mouth compressed. ''Because I'm *not* satisfied," he said. "Emma, will you become my wife?"

Emma's breath caught in her throat and her heart began to hammer in powerful strokes. She could barely force her tongue to move, to utter the astonished words, "Become your wife?"

"Yes." He made an impatient, almost angry, gesture. "Don't you see, it's the best way for me to protect you. I wouldn't let you out of my sight until we find out who this madman is. Besides..." He hesitated. "Perhaps it's indelicate of me to put it this way, but if your money is the object, the attacks would end. *I* would be the only person to profit from your demise after our marriage."

Emma felt chilled. The momentary leap her heart had taken, accelerating it to a dizzying, exhilarating speed, seemed to have exhausted her. She was angry with herself for the idiotic, foolish, unfounded, wonderful picture that had sprung into her mind the moment he uttered the words "my wife."

She lashed back, "And that's supposed to comfort me?"

He drew away as though he had been stung, and Emma thought she saw hurt in his eyes. If it had been anyone else, she would have been certain, but surely the cool, impassive Earl of Ware was impervious to such barbs. It was a moment before he said quietly, "Is that a way of saying that you don't trust me?"

Emma bowed her head and twisted her fingers together. "I'm sorry," she said, her voice nearly inaudible. "Of course I trust you. I just... I don't need to be protected like a child. It's absurd for you to suggest making a sacrifice as... as final as marriage."

"What makes you think it would be a sacrifice?" He gave a crooked smile. "I haven't made any secret of the fact that I want you badly. Marriage is obviously the only way I'm going to have you. Pretend to yourself all you wish, but I think you wouldn't find it too unpleasant."

Indignation stiffened Emma's backbone, and she smiled sweetly. "Let me see if I understand you correctly. What you're asking is that we—how did you put it?—strike a bargain. You will keep me physically safe from my unknown enemy, and in return you will have acquired my presumably willing self to frolic in bed with. And, of course, my fortune, should your side of the bargain fail. Dear me, that sounds somewhat unequal. Particularly should you tire of my body. I don't think I care for the notion that you would profit should you fail, so to speak."

"You have a devilish sharp tongue," Lord Ware remarked appreciatively. "And you know damned well that's not what I'm offering. All I'm suggesting is that we might not have a bad marriage. We certainly possess one of the principal ingredients for success. Don't we?" His eyes had that hot light in them, and he stretched one hand out toward her.

Emma stared at his hand, at the long, brown, square-tipped fingers, reaching to draw her in. Would what he suggested be so terrible? If she accepted his terms, she would become his wife, the Countess of Ware, and her passion for him would be free to bloom. She would be free in other ways as well; he was not a man to try to hem her in, or expect her to live up to some preordained role, as would so many men. She would bear his children. She would wake in the mornings with him beside her, and give him all of her that he would accept. She would have the chance to make him care for her, to return her love.

But what if he never cared? Would the pleasures of the marriage bed, and then children, be enough? How would she feel, as his wife, if she heard he had taken a mistress? Would not the pain of living with him day after day and seeing his indifference be greater than would the final gasp of agony she might feel now, refusing his offer?

"What do you say?" he asked, his voice seductively soft, confident.

She wrenched her gaze from his hand to meet his eyes, all the while shaking her head. "No. I'm sorry. I know your offer is generously meant, but . . . it's not enough. Not for me." She forced a shaky, pleading smile. "You see, I've always dreamed of marriage with a man who loved me, whom I loved, someone I could talk to, share with. A companion as well as . . . a lover. Perhaps it is no more than a fantasy, one that will never come true, but I can't settle for less." He was looking at her strangely, and she couldn't imagine what he was thinking. Before he could speak again, she said flatly, "I don't want to wed you."

His outstretched hand slowly dropped back to his side, and she saw the flash of some intense emotion flit across his face, only to be hidden with practiced ease. She wondered then, just for an instant, if he didn't already care for her more than he had admitted, at least in his own casual way. No! her realistic side cried. If Ware loved her, he would have said so. Why should he hide how he felt?

She was suddenly determined to cut the cords that held them, cleanse him of whatever obligation he felt toward her. She looked straight at him and said steadily, "I'm grateful for your concern, my lord, but it's unnecessary. I have no doubt that whoever is responsible for what happened has since discovered what a dreadful mistake has been made." She saw the growing exasperation on his face, and held up her hand. "Let me finish! I'm not such a fool that I won't be on the lookout. If somebody persists, he won't find me such an easy target the next time. I am perfectly capable of protecting myself."

The old look of mocking amusement, which could so easily become unkind, twisted his mouth. "I have never been told quite so strongly that I'm not needed—or wanted! I think, Miss Denton, that you're a fool, but we shall see." He offered her a somewhat jerky bow. "Don't expect me to attend your funeral."

"Consider yourself absolved in advance," she responded waspishly. "I wouldn't like you to suffer from guilt."

"Oh, I won't," he said. "I've done all I can ... for the moment."

Throwing this last mysterious addendum over his shoulder, he turned and was gone, leaving Emma in a profound depression. At this moment, her life seemed to have gone horridly, wretchedly astray. Somebody was trying to kill her and, much as she might like to, she couldn't quite make herself believe that it was indeed a mistake. Someone, somewhere, thought he would profit by her dying and had determined to see her in the grave.

And now the man she loved and would surely always love had asked her to become his wife, and she had refused him in such a way that he had walked away angry and humiliated. The hope of seeing him

had been all that had given spark to the season for
Emma; their encounters had been infuriating and exhilarating, uncovering emotions in her that she hadn't
known she possessed.

Oh, God, she thought, sinking down on the sofa
and pressing the heels of her hands to her aching
forehead. What was she to do? Who could want her
dead?

She had not lied to Ware. These three days, while
her shoulder throbbed with pain and she lay in bed,
she had tortured herself with possibilities, imagined
everyone she knew as a potential killer. She was not
such a fool as Ware had accused her of being; money
was the only apparent motive. And that left only two
suspects, or perhaps a third. Georgiana and Charles,
her heirs. And Papa, who might profit from his other
children's wealth, but not from Emma's. Which of
them was it? But how could it be any of them?

Their family was not a close one. Papa needed more
money; Charles envied Emma; Georgiana, it began to
seem, might even hate her. And yet, surely, there was
love as well. Papa had been kind and loving in his own
selfish way. Charles and Georgiana and Emma had
grown up together, played together, quarreled and
made up, grieved for Mama together. Could one of
them have cold-bloodedly decided to kill Emma to
become wealthy? No! It was beyond imagining. Yet
what was the alternative? There was no one else in the
world who might profit by her death, or who held a
grudge against her, or hated her.

She tried to make herself consider it reasonably.
Papa's letters had been franked in Yorkshire, although there might be ways to disguise that. Still, it
was unlikely that he was in London; too many people

might recognize him, mention his presence to Emma. No, if he was responsible, he was pulling the strings from distant Yorkshire. But why, if Papa wanted her dead, had he not seen to it at home? These attempts on her life were so obviously murderous and would draw attention and investigation should they succeed. She could so easily have had an accident at home, and the matter would have been settled in a tidy fashion. Besides... She pictured her father's face as he had said goodbye; the genuine fondness, which she returned, despite her recognition of his weaknesses. No, it could not be Papa.

And Charles... Well, Charles had perhaps the greatest motive. It was he who would inherit a mortgaged estate and no capital, who had made no secret of his resentment. Yet his resentment was that of the petulant child who still lived in the man's body. Charles had never been a good dissembler; he seemed to *want* Emma to know how he felt. She had not seen a great deal of him since they had been in London, but when they had met he had been the same as always. Surely, if he wished her dead, he would have acted differently in some way. She could not believe him to be such a good actor.

Georgiana was the one who had changed, who seemed to have forgotten the affection that had always been between them. But what could be her motive? The only way inheriting Emma's fortune might affect her was in how grand a marriage she could make, and unless she had become a very good liar indeed, she didn't greatly care for such a match. Even without a fortune she had the beauty and breeding to catch a husband who could support her adequately, and she knew it. Emma could not believe that she wished to become a wealthy spinster.

Besides, it was nearly impossible to imagine Georgiana as the culprit because of the means. How could she have hired the man? Walked up to somebody on the street? And where could she have acquired the sum needed to pay him? Emma was paying her bills, giving her only spending money. And Georgiana never left the house unsupervised. It was absurd to suppose her in the role of master criminal! Except, a niggling voice in the back of Emma's mind whispered, that she had displayed a far more determined personality than Emma had believed her to possess. Perhaps... But no. This solution to the mystery, too, did not make sense.

And yet Emma worried it over in her mind again. Perhaps her fondness for them was blinding her to the truth. Was she finding excuses for all of her family, not seeing some ruthlessness, some hate, merely because she chose not to? There was no avoiding the unpalatable fact that somebody wanted her dead. If Emma thought long and hard enough, and didn't drive herself mad first, the solution would surely reveal itself.

Perhaps it truly is a mistake, she thought. Maybe the coachman really hadn't seen her, and the near accident had simply been one of the many mishaps that occurred in a city as busy as London. And the shot... She might have been mistaken for somebody else. The shot might even have been fired by a madman, who simply wanted to shoot somebody and didn't care who it was. He might yet kill, but the chances of Emma's crossing his path again were infinitesimal. Yes, she thought eagerly. This made more sense than to suppose Georgiana—sweet, timid, gentle Georgiana—a murderer. Or Charles, or Papa.

Emma wished the earl were still here so she could explain her reasoning. Surely he would agree. But she must stop thinking of him, stop turning to him in her mind. She couldn't even let herself think of him by his first name, as she was tempted to do. His title lent the distance she needed. He had accepted her rejection as final, and there was no reason to suppose she would even see him again. She was certain that many of their past encounters had been deliberately contrived by him, and future meetings could be as easily avoided. Her depression, her sense of despair, deepened yet further, and she began the cycle again. Could it be Papa...?

FORTUNATELY for her peace of mind, the following day the entire household was scheduled to become part of a small house party at a minor estate of the Hartleys in Kent. Only at Emma's insistence did her aunt not cancel; Emma was certain the two-hour carriage ride wouldn't cause her any distress, and there was no reason to suppose she wouldn't be able to make herself as comfortable in the Hartleys' manor as she could at the Barlow town house. Actually, Emma thought it would be pleasant to escape the confines of London for a few days.

Cousin Alex had made his excuses, claiming a prior engagement, and Uncle Max had to remain in town on business until the next day. But Aunt Helen, Emma, Georgiana and a somewhat reluctant Charles planned their departure for the late afternoon, so as to arrive at about dusk, leaving plenty of time to freshen up for dinner.

The trip proved slower than they had anticipated, and dusk was beginning to settle before they found the elusive turnoff to Salcombe Manor, their destination. Lady Hartley had warned them that the gates, somewhat overgrown in ivy, were easy to miss, so the coachman was forced to rein the horses to a walk as he kept a lookout. The country lane they were on was narrow, and as shadows crept into the coach, Emma became uneasily aware that it had been a while since they had passed another traveler. It appeared that their fellow houseguests had arrived earlier in the day; the only intimation they'd had that anyone might be following the same route was an occasional glimpse of a lone horseman some distance behind.

Emma was just giving herself a stern lecture, telling herself that she was no longer a child to be frightened of the dark and that nothing could happen to her surrounded by her family, when a shot rang out just ahead, startling Aunt Helen into giving a muffled shriek. The coach swayed to a stop, and Emma could hear the coachman cursing. Charles was fumbling about, as though he thought to find a weapon, and swearing as well. A loud, rough voice could be heard outside, and the tension inside the coach had nearly reached breaking point when the door was flung open, revealing a black apparition.

With an ear-piercing scream Georgiana dove into Aunt Helen's arms, hiding her face in the ample bosom. Emma, seated beside her brother, felt his involuntary withdrawal from the horrid shape in the opening, and gave a deep shudder herself. She almost immediately perceived, however, that no ghost faced them but, rather, a man cloaked in black and with a dark cloth, which had slits cut for eyes, wrapped about

his face. The long-barreled pistol, gleaming in the uncertain light, was pointed directly at Emma, and was
as real as the man.

"You!" The barrel swung toward Charles. "Down
on your knees! Now! Hands on the seat, where I can
see them!"

Charles hesitated, whether from reluctance to assume such a humiliating posture or because he was
turning over wild plans for retaliation, Emma was
uncertain. "Charles..." she pleaded.

Silently he did the highwayman's bidding, spreading his hands wide on the leather seat. His head was
lifted defiantly and he was watching the man from the
corners of his eyes.

The pistol lifted, wavering uncertainly between
Emma and the two women crouched in the corner of
the far seat. "Take off your jewelry," he ordered in
the same coarse voice. "Throw it on the floor."

Emma unclipped the small ruby earrings she had
inherited from her mother and tossed them carefully,
hating the thought of their delicate beauty in that
man's greedy hand. She saw her aunt and sister do the
same, with Aunt Helen adding a pearl necklace.

"That's all? Where's your jewelry box?"

"We don't have one," Aunt Helen said in a surprisingly strong voice. "We're on our way to a small
house party and we won't need jewels. There are some
small items in our baggage, but nothing valuable.
Search if you like."

The slits in the mask stared unwaveringly at Aunt
Helen for a moment, then turned to Emma. "You. I
want you out."

"Me?" A chill spread through Emma's limbs, making them heavy and difficult to move. "Why do you want me?"

"No questions. Just move. Out." The pistol was leveled suggestively at her head.

Aunt Helen cried, "No! Don't go, Emma!"

The man said threateningly, "Do you want her dead?"

Emma suddenly felt sick, and she was shaken by a dry heave. Her shoulder had begun to hurt again, and her knees barely supported her as she pushed herself to her feet and stumbled toward the door, from which the highwayman had backed away. Why was he singling her out? Surely this was just a robbery. No highwayman killed if he could help it; there was no surer way to set the Bow Street Runners on him, ensuring that he would swing from the gibbet in no time. This one would be careful. They had not resisted. Perhaps he simply distrusted some outward composure he had seen in her and thought she might be hiding valuables, or wanted a temporary hostage to safeguard his departure.

Emma tripped over Charles's leg, almost vaulting headlong from the coach. She grabbed the door frame, stopping herself in time, then had to clamber clumsily from the coach.

The pistol waved her to the verge of the lane, right beside a deep ditch, beyond which was a thick growth of oaks and underbrush. Emma could see the coachman, spread-eagled on the lane beside the restless horses. He was maintaining a quiet, nonstop litany of curses, which somehow seemed an appropriate backdrop for the otherwise silent events. The cloaked figure pushed shut the door to the coach, isolating him

and Emma from the others. Darkness was still settling, although the light was sufficient for Emma to
make out the leaves on the trees and the color of the
big bay horse, a powerful brute, waiting patiently in
the lane just ahead.

As though in slow motion she saw the highwayman
turn toward her and lift his pistol, aiming it directly at
her head. A near paralysis held her in its grip, and with
horror, but somehow no surprise, she realized that he
was going to shoot her. He wanted no jewels from her;
the entire robbery had been a charade to hide its true
purpose. He was not going to say another word, not
even to explain. He would just pull the trigger, blast-
ing her into oblivion. She stared down the barrel,
wondering if she would be able to see the bullet come
out. Perhaps events were now moving so slowly that
she would be able to watch it move toward her, feel the
first crushing impact.

She saw the hand lift almost imperceptibly, then
heard the crack. She felt nothing, no pain, and she
watched unbelievingly as the pistol dropped, the man
reeled back, doubling up, then crumpled to the dusty
lane. It was another stunned moment before Emma
realized the shot had come, not from the highwayman, but from the thick copse to the side.

Emma was distantly aware of the babble from the
carriage, the thumps and cries as Aunt Helen and
Charles fought to open the door. She made no move
to assist them, however; she felt that even to bend a
finger would have been beyond her power. She ignored the fallen highwayman, who lay unmoving, and
stood staring in the direction from which the shot had
come.

At nearly the same instant, the carriage door swung wide, permitting Charles to jump out, and the greenery at the side of the road was parted to reveal the debonair figure of a gentleman, fashionably turned out from the top boots, intricately tied cravat and dark blue waistcoat to the many-caped, drab greatcoat.

The Earl of Ware leaped lightly over the ditch and strode to Emma's side. His fingers gripped her chin, forcing it up so that he could look directly into her face.

"Are you hurt?" he asked in a low voice. His fingers squeezed her chin so tightly that it nearly hurt, and she thought that his calm voice and bearing did not reflect how he truly felt. For once Lord Ware's reserve seemed shaken.

She numbly shook her head. "No. I...I don't feel anything."

Aunt Helen and Charles were upon them then, with Mrs. Barlow giving tiny cries of alarm and Charles muttering animadversions on his own inadequacy.

Ware didn't look away from Emma's face. "I was afraid his pistol would go off," he remarked, as though he were commenting on the weather.

"I...I don't think it did," Emma said with mild surprise. She suddenly found herself, absurdly, smiling. "No, I don't believe it did." She laughed, the sound loosing her paralysis. "I believe I must thank you for your most timely efforts, my lord."

"Richard."

"Richard," she amended. She tore her gaze from his to smile reassuringly at her aunt. "I'm all right, Aunt Helen, thanks to Lord Ware. We'll even recover our jewelry!"

"That man was going to shoot you!" her aunt said in shock. "I believed the other to be a mistake, but this...! I saw him! Emma, why? I don't understand!"

Nor did Emma, but her aunt's words recalled her to the necessity of observing reactions. Surely if the perpetrator were either her sister or brother, some disappointment at the failed attempt would show on their faces. Ware, she saw with a glance, seemed to have much the same idea, since he was closely regarding Charles, who stood awkwardly to one side.

Emma held out her hand to her brother, and he clasped it in a compulsive grip, relief flooding his face. The words poured out, "I'm sorry I couldn't do anything to stop him, Emma! I should have been prepared, but I didn't take the other incident seriously, and I never dreamed we'd be held up so close to London. Although, of course, he *wasn't* a highwayman. There's no excuse for my failing to protect you! I'm your brother!"

Their differing fortunes seemed, for once, to be the furthest matter from Charles's mind. Emma was willing to swear that his relief and contrition were genuine.

"There is no need to lay blame," Emma said. "I should have carried a pistol myself, but I, too, never dreamed...! However, thanks to Lord Ware, our lack of forethought was not fatal for me!"

Charles gave the earl a slightly sulky look, as though he resented his more heroic role in the affair, but civility compelled him to thrust out his hand and say, "My lord, I must thank you on my sister's behalf."

Ware's brows rose and he said dryly, "I don't believe it is necessary, as she has quite adequately thanked me herself, but..." They shook hands.

Emma had already turned to see her sister coming slowly forward, her delicate face pinched and frightened. "Emma," she said tentatively, meeting her sister's eyes. "Emma, I thought he'd shot you!" She began to cry and flung herself into Emma's arms. "Oh, Emma, I was so scared!" She abruptly pulled back to arm's length to stare wide-eyed at her sister. "You aren't hurt, are you? You're certain?"

"Quite certain," Emma said with amusement. She hugged Georgiana again. "You needn't cry, Georgy. Everything's fine now."

"But somebody's trying to *kill* you!" Georgiana cried. It was obvious that the previous attempts on Emma's life had not truly registered on her, either.

"You mean somebody *was*," the earl reminded her pointedly. "I very much fear I may have put a period to this particular malefactor." He sounded not at all perturbed at the possibility.

Emma turned slowly to look, for the first time, at the pathetic black heap in the lane. Somehow she had known from the moment the man fell that he was dead. Fearfully she whispered, "Perhaps he is someone I know."

"That would solve our problem," Lord Ware said bracingly, "but I think it doubtful. It is far more likely this is hired help. But we shall see." He knelt beside the figure and, with an abrupt motion, yanked off the mask.

Emma reluctantly searched the man's face for some sign of familiarity. His mouth hung open, and spit ran from one corner of it. Stubble disguised the shape of his jaw and cheeks, and the broad, flat face was half pressed into the dirt where he had fallen, but the glazed brown eyes, wide and staring, belonged to no one Emma had ever seen.

She made a choked sound and shook her head the smallest bit.

"Damn," Ware said, dropping the cloth back over the features, which were already freezing in death. "I hoped to just wound him. We might then have persuaded him to tell us who is behind this." He shrugged. "It seemed more imperative to prevent him from pulling that trigger."

"I appreciate your priorities," Emma agreed dryly.

"Do you think he is the same man who shot you in London?"

Emma stared down at the crumpled figure. "I can't be certain," she said slowly, "but it might have been. That man I saw so briefly, but . . . he did have brown hair, I'm sure, and . . . and was built much the same, I think."

"Then I think we can assume they *are* one and the same," the earl said, rising to his feet and brushing his hands fastidiously together.

Emma felt a flush mantling her cheeks as she looked across the dead body at her feet to the earl. "I do thank you, my . . . Richard," she said awkwardly. "And that you should help me after I assured you so repulsively that I was capable of protecting myself! You have every right to think me a complete sapskull." She paused, as the very odd fact of his presence suddenly surfaced in her mind. "How *did* you chance to be here?" she asked. "Did you follow us? Oh! It must have been you that we noticed several times on the road behind us. But why?"

Ware looked almost embarrassed. "I played a hand with your uncle at White's the other night," he explained. "Max mentioned the house party, and that you insisted on not withdrawing." He shrugged. "It seemed to me a likely time for an attack. Lonely country road, evening approaching. I'd have simply offered my escort, but that might have prevented the attempt, and I was hoping to apprehend the man." His mouth twisted as he added, "The spot was chosen particularly well, however; the woods are very thick at this point, and I was so slow in beating my way through that I very nearly failed to catch up in time."

His words had apparently been slow to register in Charles's mind, because, although the young man had been standing silent, he suddenly burst out indignantly, "Are you telling us that you were setting a trap? With my sister as bait? Not to mention the rest of us! Why, we might have all been killed!"

"Do you have a more useful suggestion?" inquired the earl politely. "Do we hire a bodyguard to protect Miss Denton day and night for the rest of her life? I feel sure she would rapidly tire of having one hang about. Besides, bullets so easily penetrate such protection."

Charles changed tack, complaining peevishly, "And was it necessary for you to beat your way through the woods? Surely it would have been less risky for you to have galloped to our rescue on the road. The impending arrival of another horseman would surely have scared that fellow off!"

"Certainly," Ware agreed. "After shooting Miss Denton. That takes so little time, you see."

There was a short silence, as all present recollected the moment when the pistol had been leveled at Emma's head. Several pairs of eyes turned to peer surreptitiously at the recumbent form of the mysterious attacker.

The moment was not allowed to become prolonged, however, as Ware somewhat impatiently remarked, "It will be completely dark very soon. I suggest you be on your way. I'm sure the other guests will be anxious for your arrival, so dinner doesn't get held back."

"But...but what about...*him*?" Emma asked. "We can't just throw a body in the ditch!"

"I'll take care of him," the earl said brusquely. "You can't arrive at a house party with a body lashed on the back of your carriage! You would be a very unpopular guest! Thor is tied up in the woods. I'll throw the body over his own horse—" he nodded toward the big animal, still waiting "—and take it to the constable in the nearest village. I think, as far as the local authorities are concerned, that we can pass it off as a highwayman who threatened to abduct Miss Denton?" He glanced about for agreement. "Very well. Miss Georgiana, let me help you up."

He gave Georgiana a hand into the carriage, then Mrs. Barlow after her, while Emma still stood rooted in place.

Finally she protested, "But where are you going tonight? Aren't you coming with us to Salcombe Manor? I'm sure you'd be welcome."

There was little doubt that Lady Hartley would eagerly welcome the addition to her guest list of such an eligible bachelor. The story of tonight's doings would set all the young ladies fluttering, in any case, and to have the hero of the story among them would be all that was required to make the party an enviable success.

But Ware was shaking his head. "No, I have engagements in town. I'll put up at the local hostelry and ride back in the morning." He nodded at the body. "This will surely be at least a temporary setback in someone's plans. I feel sure you will be safe for the remainder of the week. Once back in London, however..." Just before he assisted her, too, into the carriage, the earl gave Emma a last penetrating look. "Emma, use this time to *think*! Everyone's luck runs out eventually. Yours has stood by you very well thus far."

As she sank back against the leather squabs, heard the crack of the whip and the creak of the harness, felt the coach lurch and sway as it again began its slow journey, Emma carried the vivid picture in her head of Ware's face: the harsh, angular lines barely visible, the dark blue eyes nearly black in the failing light, and yet some intensity leaping out at her, compelling her, giving her strength.

Emma sighed and allowed her eyelids to close, shutting out the sight of her companions, all staring at her as though they had found a stranger in their midst.

CHAPTER NINE

WHEN EMMA AWOKE the following morning, she lay staring up at the pink silk canopy, which stretched over the enormous four-poster. She was not anxious to rise and make her way to the breakfast room, where she would immediately become the continuing object of speculation, awe and even jealousy. She could not have drawn more attention had she risen from the dead.

She groaned and rolled over to bury her face in the cloyingly soft pillow. How was she to bear two more days of this? She had never dreamed that others would see Lord Ware's rescue as tantamount to a declaration. Did they think he should have ridden by, ignoring her predicament, so as not to compromise himself? Of course, they had guessed that he had followed her, but Emma could only be thankful they didn't know why. Although most knew of her gunshot wound, general opinion seemed to be that Emma had simply been unfortunate enough twice to be in the wrong place at the wrong time. No one had even imagined the truth.

But what was the truth? she wondered. She was now unswervingly certain that neither her sister nor brother was guilty, and that both would be horrified if they knew she had even suspected them.

So whom did that leave? Papa? He had been an unlikely suspect from the outset, and this incident eliminated him as surely as it had Georgiana and Charles. He would have had no way of knowing about the invitation to Salcombe Manor. Whoever had planned this ambush had known Emma would drive into it, and when.

If either Georgiana or Charles had been married, or even promised... This thought, so obvious, brought Emma upright in bed. There was Lydia Stonor, who was certainly seen a good deal in Charles's company... but could she be so certain of him that she would try to ensure him an inheritance? They had been acquainted such a short time that it was unlikely he had yet made her an offer. Besides, Mrs. Stonor gave every indication of having ample means of her own. Nonetheless, the time had come to cease depending on mere speculation and find out for certain. Uncle Max could be depended on to set inquiries in motion.

For now, that left Georgiana, who, now Emma came to think the matter through, did give every indication of a girl in love with someone she knew her family would not like. There was her sulkiness, the refusal to encourage any of the eligible suitors who flocked around her, the girlish giggles with Julia, the obvious unhappiness. Yet how could it be? She was always properly chaperoned, usually by Aunt Helen and Emma, sometimes by Lady Hartley, who could be depended on to discourage ineligible gentlemen. If this unknown man had confidence that he could win Georgiana's hand, or persuade her to elope with him, he must have cause, which meant clandestine meetings.

Emma's brow furrowed, but then cleared without delay. The answer leaped into her mind so quickly that she could only believe suspicions had already been gathering there. Of course, it had to be those morning walks that Georgiana so anticipated, and from which she often returned home in almost frantically high spirits, which generally plummeted before the first social occasion of the day. It was Julia Hartley's maid who accompanied the girls, and the maid was young enough to be persuaded that secret meetings were romantic. And Julia, of course, was just the girl to encourage Georgiana in such an unwise adventure.

Emma's first impulse was to leap out of bed and march into her sister's room to confront her. Common sense came to her rescue, however; Georgiana was certain to deny that she was meeting anyone, and if she fancied herself in love, would refuse to believe the man might be trying to murder her sister.

No, the wiser course for Emma to pursue would be to wait until they had returned to London (she comforted herself by recalling that the earl had as good as promised she would be secure until then), and then surreptitiously follow Georgiana and Julia on their walk. She would confront the man, for her own satisfaction, then set the Bow Street Runners on him. Whether they were able to prove his culpability or not, he would know his chances of marrying Georgiana had been destroyed, and Emma's fortune would lose its interest for him.

Having such a sensible plan was an immediate comfort to Emma, and she was able to rise from the ridiculously soft bed in a more carefree frame of mind. She would simply pity those who made remarks with veiled malice; Emma's adventures had obviously brought home to them how very dull were their own lives.

SHE SUCCEEDED in enduring the next two days, primarily by clinging to the older members of the party, who were less inclined to find a dangerous adventure something to envy. But it was an enormous relief to be once more resident in town, although, with the moment of truth at hand, Emma found herself feeling somewhat apprehensive. She could not allow herself to be such a coward, however, as to withdraw from the chase! Who would take her place? What if she set the Bow Street Runners on the trail of some perfectly innocuous young gentleman who had foolishly allowed himself to be persuaded into secret meetings? No, Emma must meet the man herself, face-to-face.

It was no surprise to anyone when, the morning after their return to London, Julia arrived, her maid in tow, and requested the pleasure of Georgiana's companionship for a walk through Green Park. It even seemed to Emma, although she knew she might well be oversensitive, that the two girls exchanged a significant look before making their excuses and departing.

Emma waited only until they had started across the square before calling for her maid, gathering her pelisse from the chair in the drawing room where she had bundled it, and setting out.

Neither girl glanced over her shoulder, or evinced the slightest interest in passersby, so Emma had no difficulty keeping them in sight.

Green Park was not a fashionable place to stroll, particularly at this early hour of the morning. Most of those enjoying the pleasantly sunny day were children attended by their nursemaids, who used the time to gossip. Therefore, the tall, dark, fashionably dressed gentleman loitering near some playing toddlers drew the eye. He was a man who looked as though he should have been waving a saber and shouting commands from the slanting deck of a pirate ship. Emma would have expected the nursemaids to be hovering near their charges, darting suspicious looks at the intruder among them. Instead, he might as well have been a tree for all the attention he drew. He was clearly a familiar figure. This was not the first time Sir James Finkirk had waited here for Miss Georgiana Denton.

Emma watched as Julia and the maid turned to begin a slow walk about the perimeter of the park, while Georgiana moved with eager steps toward Sir James, whose face lit up at the sight of his beloved. Emma felt cold inside. She had guessed that she might find Sir James at the end of this walk, but had prayed it might not be so. The way he had smiled down at her sister that evening at the ball had stirred something in Emma also. Perhaps it was regret; she wanted him, for Georgiana's sake, to be more worthy than he was. At the same time she had known, remembering his swarthy face, that he was far different from the callow youth she had hoped her sister was innocently meeting; Sir James was a man who might dare much. Emma thought it was quite possible that he *was* capable of arranging a murder, if it was to his and Georgiana's advantage.

Emma shook herself, as a dog might, then turned to Betty.

"Wait here," she said fiercely. "I'm going to speak to them."

She wasted no time in intercepting Julia and sending her home with sharp words ringing in her ears.

"I know very well what your role in this whole affair has been, and so will your mother very shortly. I hold you responsible for encouraging Georgiana! She would never have dared act so on her own. Nor would she have had the opportunity! And you," she added, turning a blistering look on the maid, "have been negligent as well! Lady Hartley trusted you to have more sense than two foolish girls!"

After Julia had departed in tears, accompanied by the equally frightened maid, Emma advanced with militant strides toward the illicit pair, who remained entirely unconscious of her approach, so absorbed in each other were they.

At her precipitate arrival Sir James lifted his head, his dark eyes narrowing with recognition, while Georgiana spun around with a gasp. Upon seeing Emma, she quailed into the circle of Sir James's arm, one hand pressed to her mouth.

Sir James spoke up immediately, sounding remarkably cool considering the circumstances. "You have every right to be angry," he said. "And you're certainly entitled to an explanation; this is not how—or where—" he cast a distasteful glance at a screaming child "—convention dictates Miss Georgiana and I should meet."

"It's so kind of you to concede me the right to protect my sister!" Emma retorted with withering sarcasm. "And Georgiana's aunt and uncle prefer that she not meet you at all, in any location. You cannot be unaware of how they feel, or you would not have resorted to a clandestine rendezvous. Surely you can see that Georgiana is too young to be encouraged in an action that could so easily destroy her reputation!''

There was a hot flush beneath the tan on his cheeks. "You misunderstand. It was not I who insisted on meeting thus, but your sister. It is my desire to make Georgiana my wife, and I would have preferred to approach your father at once, but you must see that I couldn't run counter to your sister's wishes, no matter how painful to me they are. I want the world to know she is mine. Do you think I like knowing half the bachelors in London are making sheeps' eyes at her every evening? Such secrecy has been repugnant to me!'' He broke off, the force of his feelings apparently overcoming him.

Emma lashed back, "You call her yours! How can you believe you might be acceptable to Papa? Your reputation as a fortune hunter precedes you, sir!''

His flush darkened still further. "I was never that,'' he said vehemently. "I can't deny that I've lived beyond my means, and that I had creditors with cause to reproach me, but I would never have married to remedy my situation. In any event, your sister has no fortune.''

Emma stared hard at him. "I, however, do,'' she said. "And Georgiana is my heiress.''

She could have sworn he was bewildered. "But she will never inherit from you. No tradesman would consider giving us credit on such an expectation. You are a very young woman and will surely marry and have children. Your fortune can hold no advantage for me. We would never hang on your sleeve!''

Understanding was creeping into Georgiana's face, and her eyes widened still further. "Emma!'' she whispered. "You cannot think . . . How *can* you think such a thing?" Her voice rose hotly on the last words.

Sir James looked from one to the other sister, his puzzlement evident. "Think what, Georgiana? What is it your sister believes?"

Georgiana did not remove her accusing gaze from Emma. "Is that what you suspect, Emma?" she asked quietly.

Emma bit her lip and nodded. She had hoped to hide her suspicions from her sister until they were confirmed; she had no wish to hurt Georgiana. It was with regret, therefore, that she said, "I'm sorry, Georgy. Somebody *is* trying to kill me. It seemed to make sense, you see."

"Perhaps someone might care to explain," Sir James suggested, his tone ironic. "I am beginning to develop a very uneasy feeling."

"Emma thinks you hired someone to kill her," Georgiana announced flatly.

His mouth literally dropped open for a second; then he began to stutter, "Kill her! Are you mad? I've heard some absurd accusations before, but this . . .! What would make you think—"

When neither girl responded, he finally took a deep breath and looked straight at Georgiana. "Surely *you* don't believe such a thing?"

Georgiana smiled up at him, her expression soft and warm, as loving and trusting as a child's. "Of course I don't, silly! And if Emma knew you as I do, she wouldn't, either."

Reassured as to his beloved's faith, Sir James turned his attention to Emma. "Perhaps you might enlighten me as to why you do believe it. In fact, you might tell me why you think anyone is trying to have you killed!''

Emma's gaze faltered as she felt her certainty begin to slip away; perhaps she had been infected by Georgiana's loving confidence. Matters were not coming out as Emma had intended them to. She had imagined Georgiana hanging her head in shame, with Sir James defiantly confessing his vile intentions.

Perhaps it would be enough if she told Sir James that Georgiana was no longer her heiress, and let him walk away. She felt no powerful need to see him punished, if he was guilty. But what if she died because she had mistakenly believed her enemy to be him and allowed herself to feel safe? No, she needed to know for certain, one way or the other.

Emma said calmly, "Surely, Sir James, Georgiana has told you about my 'accidents.'"

"No. That is, yes, she mentioned a near mishap with a coach, but as you weren't hurt I didn't think that anybody gave the matter much thought. There are many careless people about, you know, and with London so crowded..." He shrugged. "An occasional accident is the result."

"And do you think it was carelessness," Emma inquired sarcastically, "that sent a bullet through my shoulder when I was riding in the middle of the day in Hyde Park? It seems a very peculiar place to come across a stray bullet!"

There was a little silence; then he said, "No, I doubt that was carelessness. But the other might still have been. Please don't think I'm belittling your fear, but it might well be that the man who shot you was a lunatic, who didn't even know who you were." The words were nearly an echo of Emma's reasoning when it was still possible for her to delude herself.

Georgiana said, "Yes, we thought something of the kind also, but then...I was going to tell you today. We joined a house party at one of Lord Hartley's estates in Kent, and we were held up on the way by a man in a mask?"

"A highwayman?" he said in quick alarm. "I can't bear to think of you in danger!"

"*She* was in no danger," Emma interjected dryly. "It was me he forced out of the coach."

"He was going to shoot Emma!" Georgiana chimed in. "He held the pistol pointed straight at her head. I couldn't look!"

"And then what happened?" he impatiently urged. "Obviously he didn't succeed."

"The Earl of Ware rescued Emma," she said dramatically. "He crept through the woods and shot the man, just before he could pull the trigger! The earl killed him," she added with relish.

"Under the circumstances," Sir James observed, "that was a pity." There was a short silence as he heard his own choice of words; then a horrified look spread across his lean face. "That didn't come out precisely as I intended it," he said hastily. "It's just that a conversation with the man might have proved most instructive."

"Yes," Emma agreed. "Lord Ware said much the same. He would have preferred to wound the man."

Emma wondered if she and Georgiana were telling Sir James anything he didn't already know. Then she realized that, even if he had hired the highwayman, he must have been mystified as to his fate. The local authorities had doubtless buried the man without making any great effort to ascertain his identity. To his employer, it must seem as though he had vanished from the earth.

As though he had read her mind, Sir James went on, "I can readily understand why you think your life is in danger. What I fail to understand is why you suspect me in particular."

"I should think that was obvious," Emma said with contempt, all the while watching his changing expressions with close attention. "Whom should I suspect? To the best of my knowledge, I have never made an enemy. I am, however, the recent heiress to a sizable fortune. I simply asked myself who would profit from my death. Perhaps I should tell you that I have written a new will, and Georgiana is no longer my beneficiary. I'm sorry, Georgy," she added gently.

Georgiana's white brow creased. "You don't think I . . . ?" she began.

"Of course she doesn't," Sir James reassured her. "It is *my* evil intentions your sister is sensibly guarding against. There is only one difficulty," he said to Emma. "I have never even wished for your death, far less taken steps to put such a desire into execution. Even were I poor as a church mouse, I would not do such a thing. I had my fill of killing on the Peninsula."

"Sir James was one of the duke's aides," Georgiana said proudly.

He ignored this irrelevancy. "I cannot expect you to place any great faith in my word. The fact is, however, that I do not need your fortune. If Georgiana becomes my wife, I will have all I could wish for."

"You enjoy having creditors hound you?" inquired Emma with skepticism. "Knowing your suit cannot be acceptable to Papa?"

"I have paid my debts," he said stiffly. "And I am perfectly able to support Georgiana in comfort. I am determined to make my case to your father."

Emma had a peculiar sensation, as though the ground were shifting under her feet. "Have I misjudged you?" she asked slowly.

"You had no way of knowing. You see," he explained, "this past winter I inherited my great-uncle's estate. It's not grand, but there's a snug little manor in Shropshire, with adequate room for a family, and a well-run farm. There's even enough in funds to provide for extras. But Georgiana doesn't think it's enough to satisfy your father," he finished.

Emma looked in astonishment at her sister. "Georgiana, what makes you think Papa would object? He wants only what will make you happy!"

"I once heard you and Papa talking about how none of the boys back home would do for me," Georgiana said. "Papa was positively cruel to Augustus Wenley when he tried to kiss me that time. I assumed it was because you all wanted me to marry someone really wealthy. You've said so many things since we came to London, Emma, as though you had such expectations! I thought Papa and Charles required some sort of generous settlement."

"Georgiana, you goose," Emma exclaimed. "They don't expect you to provide for them! Papa's never even asked me for assistance!" This was not quite true, but she thought a small white lie suitable to the occasion. "All any of us have hoped for," she went on, "is that you would make a respectable match with

THE IMPERILED HEIRESS 173

a gentleman who could provide adequately for you and would care for you. I sometimes imagined, because you're so beautiful, that you might marry high, but I neither expect it nor care whether you do. I just want you to be happy, Georgy! I brought you to London only so you could meet a man you would be able to love. We didn't want you to settle for a silly boy like Augustus Wenley merely because there was no one else."

"Do you mean that?" Georgiana's face began to glow.

"Of course I do," Emma said staunchly. "If what Sir James claims is true, then I feel sure Papa will bestow his blessing, and you know I will. And also..." She gave Sir James a troubled look. "It begins to look as though I owe you an apology. To suspect you of such a heinous crime as attempted murder with so little reason is unforgivable. You must be very angry with me."

"Of course I'm not," he exclaimed. "You didn't know me, and so had no reason to trust me. In fact, to the contrary! And I think your reasoning was very sound." He hesitated. "Has it occurred to you to wonder where my disqualification leaves you? If it is true that someone is determined to have you dead, you *must* find out who that is. Perhaps some imagined slight, far in the past, a worker let go..." The dissatisfaction he felt at these explanations sounded clearly in his voice.

Emma ruefully agreed. "Yes, clearly I need to think it through again."

After a moment he went on, "I'm sure you've considered it, but was this last attack one that had to be planned beforehand? Anybody could have followed you to Hyde Park, but holding up a coach is another matter! Was it a lonely road, where the man could be certain of remaining undisturbed? And how did he know your coach from others that might have passed?"

"I am certain it was somebody who knew our plans in detail," Emma said flatly. "That's one of the reasons I suspected you. I felt sure Georgiana would have told you when we intended to travel."

"But I didn't!" the younger girl exclaimed. "The last time I saw James was before you were shot, and I had forgotten all about the invitation to Salcombe Manor. He was leaving for Newmarket, and we haven't met since. So you see, he didn't know."

"It's true," he agreed. "I had no idea you were even out of town. In fact, I've been waiting every morning for the past three days for Georgiana to walk here in the park, half afraid she had decided not to come again."

"Please, you don't need to explain," said Emma in mortification. "I must ask your pardon for holding such dreadful suspicions."

Before he could respond, Georgiana said, "Emma, how did you know I was meeting anybody at all? I thought I'd been so careful! You must have followed us today."

"And why did you believe it to be me?" Sir James asked.

Emma explained. "I became suspicious because you've changed so much, Georgiana. Your spirits have leapfrogged up and down, and were generally only high after these walks. In fact, it seemed to me you enjoyed walking far too much for a young lady who had never cared much for exercise."

"I've been horrid to you, haven't I?" Georgiana exclaimed, tears springing readily to her vivid blue eyes. "I just couldn't help it! I wanted so badly to tell you about Sir James, but I've been afraid to. As long as no one knew, I could at least hope. I'm so glad you've found us out."

"Was it Sir James you met at Vauxhall that night?"

"I knew that was a mistake," he muttered.

"It was romantic!" Georgiana said rebelliously. "I wanted to walk with you, not that silly boy! All he wants to do is pay me absurd compliments, or else brag about hitting someone at that dreadful Jackson's, as though I should care for such fustian."

Emma had to smile at this picture of the average young sporting gentleman. She said, "That is precisely why I felt sure you were meeting Sir James. You spoke about *him* in a far different way than you did about any of the other gentlemen you met. It seemed to me that Sir James looked at you in a very particular way as well."

The lovers exchanged shy smiles.

Emma turned impulsively toward Sir James. "Why don't you walk home with us now, Sir James, and speak to Uncle Max? I can explain the circumstances to him, and I'm certain he would be happy to act in Papa's stead for the moment, although, of course, he couldn't authorize a betrothment. But he could hear in more detail about your estate, and perhaps even go to see it with you. If *he* writes a recommendation to Papa, there would be no difficulty at all. You must be anxious to have it settled."

"Very," he agreed, with the tiniest tremor in his voice. He looked down at Georgiana with such overwhelming emotion in his eyes that Emma had to swallow and glance away in embarrassment. How desperately she wished Lord Ware would look at her with such love in his eyes! She shook her head, banishing the vision. It was hopeless to dream so foolishly! Instead, she should be occupying her mind with something more immediate: If it was not Sir James who wished her dead, who could it be?

CHAPTER TEN

EMMA LAY AWAKE long into the night, swathed in the cocoon of bedclothes, hearing the occasional clatter of hooves on the cobblestones outside, or the far-off cries of the watchman. She thought of the day that had just passed, and of what it meant for her own future. Today's trail had proved to be false, but she had seen signs that pointed another way. She could not give up the hunt now.

That afternoon Uncle Max and Sir James had remained closeted in the study for over an hour, but when they emerged, Uncle Max was obviously satisfied.

He confided privately to Emma that he thought the match to be all they could have hoped for. "There was a time," he confessed, "that I thought Georgiana might look as high as she wished for in a husband, but obviously she is indifferent to such success. Besides, I think we must admit she has not taken well with the ton. Although her manners are pretty, she displays a lack of animation, of confidence, that gives her an appearance of shallowness." He glanced quickly at Emma and hastened to add, "Falsely, of course. It is merely that she is shy. It may be, too," he added thoughtfully, "that it was unfortunate she had a sister to be contrasted with, as *you* possess in abundance the very qualities Georgiana lacks. Julia, also.... But that is all by the way now, isn't it? I think Sir James and she will be well content with each other, and that is far more important than worldly success. I'm convinced Finkirk has his affairs in order, and I know of nothing else to his discredit; in fact, I understand Wellington thinks very highly of him and has always regretted his...difficulties. And Georgiana looks very happy, does she not?''

"Yes, indeed! You will write Papa on their behalf, then?''

"I think it would be best. Perhaps your father could meet Sir James in Shropshire for a tour of inspection, and then, if all is approved, they could come straight to London for the wedding. I see no cause for delay, do you?''

"None whatsoever! They are certainly eager, and I have no doubt Georgiana knows her mind. For her to have been brave enough to meet Sir James against our wishes certainly argues for that." She hesitated. "It is Charles who concerns me now.''

"I've been meaning to speak to you about him," Uncle Max said, somewhat to her surprise. "Tell me, do you suspect his feelings for this widow to be serious?''

Emma stared at her uncle. "I don't know," she said at last. "I feel certain that he imagines himself in love with her, but whether he is actually considering her as a wife I haven't any idea. He's far from forthcoming to me, you know. We have never been close.''

"I had noticed some resentment," he admitted. He picked up an inlaid brass paperweight from his desk and began to fiddle with it, tossing it from hand to hand.

"Is there something I should know about?" Emma asked quietly. "It's not like you to... well, to fuss."

He grinned ruefully. "No, it isn't, is it? But then, Alex has given me little cause for worry. Not that he's perfect, mind, but he hasn't yet gotten into any difficulties from which he couldn't extricate himself. I wouldn't concern myself about Charles, either, except that your father isn't in town. I'm wondering if I should speak to the boy."

"You must know more than I do," Emma said. "I've seen remarkably little of Charles and only met Mrs. Stonor on two occasions. I've been uneasy because of their obvious intimacy, and because we know so little of her."

"You were quite right to be uneasy," her uncle said bluntly. "After talking to you, I did some checking. I found nothing disreputable, but our dashing widow is not at all what she seems. Apparently Mr. Stonor was a well-to-do cit, who, unfortunately for his wife, made some poor investments shortly before he died. Her father is evidently a farmer—sheep, I believe—respectable, but that's all. I think our Mrs. Stonor is an ambitious woman."

"Because of her relationship with Charles?"

He made no effort to evade her question. "Because of her attempt to undertake a season at all. From what I can gather, she hasn't the funds to pay for it; she is gambling on her ability to make an advantaged marriage. And it may be not only money she seeks; your brother is heir to a title, after all. What's more, with your backing, he's living in high style. It's possible she doesn't realize in what financial straits he stands." He shrugged. "Perhaps she is even genuinely fond of him. But whatever her motivation, she won't do for Charles." He gave Emma a shrewd look. "Would it do any good for me to talk to him, or would it set his back up?"

Emma was not as surprised by her uncle's story as she might have been. Although her worries on the subject of Lydia Stonor had been unformed, vague, based on little more than her own instinctive dislike of the woman, they had been present nonetheless. And, of course, the attempts on Emma's life had given her cause to view many people with suspicion.

"I fear Charles would be angry," she said slowly. "He hates to be reproved for his conduct and would think you were interfering where you didn't have cause or authority. Still, he knows the state of Papa's finances and that if he hopes to hold on to Denton Hall he must marry money. It is difficult for me to believe that Charles would knowingly jeopardize his own future. So perhaps a hint..."

Uncle Max set the paperweight squarely on his desk, and his eyes met Emma's. "That should present no difficulty. And if it doesn't appear to serve the purpose, I *will* have words with him, whether it stiffens his back or not, and threaten to bring Harry running. Charles won't take a chance on having his inheritance, such as it is, cut off."

Emma agreed and a moment later continued on to her room, mulling over the talk in her mind as she went. Her thoughts, of course, were running along rather different lines from her uncle's. Lydia's background confirmed her willingness to gamble for stakes high enough to be worth the uncertainty—and her reasons for wanting Emma dead.

But what was Emma to do about it? She lay in bed, as the night crept on, trying to plan. Would anybody at all believe her if she explained her reasoning? For, once again, all she had on her side was logic, not evidence. She could not understand why the same logic had not immediately made itself felt to Uncle Max when they discussed Mrs. Stonor. She guessed that he was chivalric and old-fashioned enough to have difficulty in bringing himself to imagine a woman committing such a brutal crime as murder. To consider Lydia in the role of a suspect had apparently not even occurred to him, although he was able to regard with a cynical eye her motive in pursuing Charles.

But even if Uncle Max *would* listen, what could they do? The Bow Street Runners would have difficulty collecting evidence at this late date. The man who had actually pulled the trigger—and, in all likelihood, had held the reins of the thundering coach—was in the grave, disintegrating into the earth and therefore past identifying.

What if Emma called on Lydia and said, "I know you have tried to have me killed. Others know it as well. If anything happens to me now, however accidental it appears, you will be held responsible. No inheritance will come to Charles, and every attempt will be made to prove that you are guilty of murder"— would this be enough? Would Emma then be safe, or would Lydia Stonor think herself cleverer than Emma, and believe she could still find a way?

The image of this conversation intrigued Emma. Could she lure Lydia into an indiscretion? Of course, that would accomplish nothing, she immediately realized. There would be no witnesses, or at least none who were not Lydia's confederates, because if there were, the widow would not commit the indiscretion.

What was needed was for Lydia to make an incriminating statement, and for Emma to have another witness present. A trap; the word slid into her mind. She imagined herself a poacher, setting her trap in the dark of the night in a secret place, where it would be discovered by no one but the victim, and then only after it was sprung. Yes, the idea had merit, but how was it to be accomplished?

She would certainly need an accomplice of her own. Under other circumstances, Uncle Max would have been the obvious person to whom to turn, but Emma knew that he would never consent to a plan that involved putting her in any danger, however remote. Charles? Of course not. It was a pity that Papa was not in town, for this was precisely the kind of adventurous undertaking he would revel in; but it was Emma's own doing that placed him so far away. She could not afford to wait until he arrived in London, which might be weeks away.

Emma briefly considered taking Sir James into her confidence. He seemed to possess the necessary sense, as well as an admirable air of possession, and, of course, he would shortly be a relative by marriage. Reluctantly, however, she had to abandon the idea; he had been her chief suspect until that morning, and he knew it, which would make his sudden promotion to colleague somewhat awkward. Besides, he was so little acquainted with Emma that he might well think her idea mad.

Emma tossed restlessly in the bed, wishing fretfully that she had possessed the foresight to become, if not married, at least betrothed. She had never before realized how useful a husband could be. Perhaps she could tell Mr. Linley that she had changed her mind, then, once this affair was finished, change it once again. But, of course, this was impractical. Aside from the inherent dishonesty of it, which was naturally repugnant to Emma, Mr. Linley wouldn't do. If he had been the sort of gentleman who would do, she might have agreed to marry him.

All of this left her with the one individual who would do admirably, but whom she was most reluctant to ask. She knew Lord Ware was not so chivalric as to balk at placing a woman in danger, and she suspected that, if he agreed with her reasoning, he would think her idea an excellent one. He had already used her as bait, without her consent, in a similar scheme. He had the standing, as well, that would enable him to call upon the Runners, and Emma felt sure they would jump to his bidding. The Earl of Ware would be the perfect partner in this adventure.

But how could she humble herself by asking his assistance? Did etiquette permit one to ask a favor—and such a favor!—from a man whose offer of marriage one had so recently refused? She would be enormously in his debt! But he had already shown, despite her rejection of his suit, that he was determined to protect her. Emma told herself she need have no qualms about turning to him. She could send a note around asking him to call. Then, daringly, she decided it would be better if she called on him. If he came here, they would chance being interrupted by

Aunt Helen or Georgiana or any of the constant stream of morning callers. And Tompkins would doubtless be leaning toward the keyhole.

THE FOLLOWING MORNING, at half-past ten, Emma slipped out the side door of the house. Dressed in a drab brown merino gown, with an old brown cloak that she had found hanging in the servants' quarters draped over her shoulders, she knew she would be taken for a maid about her mistress's business. The day was cool enough that she was able to wear the hood to cover her gleaming hair and occasion no comment. She wanted to melt into her environment, not appear furtive.

She had chosen to walk the mile to the earl's mansion, rather than attempt to secure a hackney. She had been tempted to send a lower footman to do her bidding, but feared he would promptly inform Tompkins, who would as speedily report to his mistress. To a countrywoman such as herself, the walk would merely give her a chance to stretch her legs and plan what she would say to the earl.

The one difficulty she had foreseen was in being admitted to his presence. Unchaperoned ladies did not commonly call upon a single gentleman, particularly at this hour of the morning. Worse yet, her appearance would not impress Ware's butler, who might refuse even to send a message to his master.

Nonetheless, she walked up the broad steps to the heavy front door of the earl's town residence with every appearance of confidence, and let the brass knocker drop. The door swung open immediately, revealing a severely dressed butler, whose astonishment was all too evident.

He recovered quickly, however, and said icily, as he began to close the door in her face, "If it's work you're seeking, try the back door. You'd do better not to ape your betters!"

Emma held out an imperative hand. "I wish to speak to his lordship," she said authoritatively. "My name is Miss Denton. He will know me."

The door, open only a crack, seemed to hesitate in its passage, then swung wider again. The man regarded Emma skeptically, but stood aside and said, "You'd best come in."

Once in the marble-floored foyer, Emma pushed the hood back, hoping the smooth swirl of hair her maid had deftly fashioned into a Grecian knot was still intact. She had counted on the fashionable style to help convince the butler of her legitimacy, although her accent no doubt helped.

She turned to face him, holding her chin high, and said, "Will you please inform Lord Ware that Miss Denton desires to speak to him? I trust he *is* still at home?" A horrible feeling overtook her. What if he had risen early and was already gone, perhaps to one of his clubs, or, worse yet, on his way to Newmarket, as she knew many gentlemen were?

"His lordship is at home," the butler said woodenly, dispelling her worst anxiety. There was another pause; then he added reluctantly, "I'll inform him of your presence." This was accompanied by another doubting look, which Emma met with an outward show of composure. "Will you wait in here, miss?"

"Here" was an elegant drawing room, with drapes in forest green pulled back by gold tassels from the gracefully proportioned bow windows. The walls were the palest of sea-foam green, and the delicate carved moldings were a clean white. Emma hurried toward a gilt-framed looking glass to inspect her hair, which she was relieved to see had, for once, chosen to conform to her wishes. She pulled the cloak from her shoulders and laid it across the back of a green velvet sofa, wishing she had not carried her camouflage to the extent of wearing such an ugly gown. She couldn't even recollect why she had brought this drab housekeeping gown to London at all.

She was just beginning to panic and wish she had chosen the more proper course of sending a note around to the earl when the door opened and Ware strolled in. Emma was alarmed to see that he wore riding clothes, but he had not yet donned his coat. The informality of his shirt sleeves helped create an instant air of intimacy from which Emma recoiled.

"I'd like to say how charming you look this morning, but . . ." He paused, insolently studying her from head to foot.

Emma blushed but held her chin proudly high. "I did not wish to draw attention," she said.

"Wisely," he agreed. "I must compliment you. Your gown is certainly a success in that respect. Please, have a seat. Would you care for refreshments? You must be fatigued from your walk. I gather you *did* walk?"

"I am not so weak that occasionally putting one foot before the other fatigues me!" Emma said impatiently. "And no, I don't care for refreshments."

"Just as well," he murmured. "Wiley was not at all convinced as to your identity. It might lower his dignity to wait on you."

Emma turned away to hide her burning cheeks. Was the earl mocking her? Would her action in coming here unchaperoned make him hold her in disgust?

"Did you believe it really was me?" she asked in a low voice.

"Naturally!" He sounded amused. "What other lady of my acquaintance would dare stride boldly up to my front door and ask to speak to me?" The amusement was abruptly gone as he added, "Or is in a situation where such straits are necessary. I assume this *is* related to your present difficulties."

"Yes." She swung back to face him, self-consciousness forgotten. "I think I know who it is that wishes me dead."

His gaze sharpened at her dramatic announcement, but his tone made light of the import of her claim, as he remarked, "Good for you! I knew self-preservation would prove a powerful spur. So, do you plan to keep me in suspense? Shall we make it a guessing game?"

Emma bit her lip. "Do you take nothing seriously?" she asked. "Do you even care?"

His blue eyes met hers, and it was as though curtains had been drawn back from windows, revealing the naked anger that burned within. "I care," he responded quietly.

Emma did not look away from that scorching gaze. "I believe it to be Lydia Stonor," she said. "Do you know her?"

In an instant the customary cool mask had settled back over his features, leaving them imperturbable as always. "Yes, I've seen her," he said, sounding thoughtful. "She's a beautiful woman, although not quite in the usual style. I understand her hooks are firmly in your brother's flesh, although he doesn't appear to be fighting. Yes, it certainly looks as though she will be the next Viscountess Denton. And I assume he is your heir?" He took her silence for assent and went on in the same conversational tone, "I understand your logic, but do you have more cause to suspect her? Is it possible there is a man who stands in the same position to your sister?"

Emma's back stiffened and she challenged, "Need it be a man? Are you unwilling to believe a woman capable of such perfidy? If so, I am wasting my time in discussing this with you!"

"Kindly cease attributing me with the prejudices and motives of others," he said coldly. "I am merely attempting to ascertain how well grounded your suspicion is."

Grudgingly, Emma said, "I apologize." She sat in a silk-covered chair and watched as Ware abandoned his relaxed stance before the small fire burning on the grate and walked across the room to stare out the window. She was conscious again of how easily he moved, and her body quickened at her awareness. She had to fight the mixture of hostility and longing that always gripped her in the earl's presence and made sparks so quick to rise between them. Perhaps coming here today had been a mistake.

At length she mastered herself enough to describe her suspicions of Sir James, and the outcome of that confrontation. "So you see," she concluded, "he truly appears to have no need for my fortune. You will no doubt think me naive, but I believed his assurances."

"Finkirk and your sister?" Ware had turned so his back was to the window, and the light formed a halo about him. "I know him well and cannot imagine him choosing a decorative doll for a wife!"

"You are misjudging Georgiana," Emma said after a pause, adding with difficulty, "as I, too, have done. She is . . . different with him, comes out of herself more easily, is more confident. You would scarcely know her. They suit each other very well."

"I must accept your word." He sounded unconvinced. "And no, I do not think you naive. If you had consulted me . . . But, of course, you could not be certain it was Sir James at all until you had followed your sister. I have been acquainted with him for a great number of years; we served together on the duke's staff. I knew of his inheritance and could have told you. Admittedly, however, it is a modest competence, no more, and many people would not be satisfied, although I believe Finkirk has always been greatly interested in modern farming methods and will doubtless be completely content tinkering about on the land. I will not say he does not have it in him to be a murderer, as I saw him kill, but to do so in a secretive way, to hire another to do the work for him, and for the victim to be a woman . . . No, I could not believe it."

Emma nodded. "I am glad to hear you confirm my thoughts, because, of course, there is no way to be certain. He could simply be a most plausible liar, who is using Georgiana. However, you can see, in part, why I believe it *must* be Mrs. Stonor. There are only four people with a motive that I am aware of: Sir James, Mrs. Stonor, Charles and Georgiana. And I know you observed, as I did, Charles's and Georgiana's faces at my near escape in Kent. It is impossible to believe either engineered the scheme!''

"Yes, I agree. Besides..." He hesitated, then resumed. "Also—forgive me—but I cannot credit either with the will or intellect to plan so effectively, and ruthlessly, for a more advantageous future. Your brother, in particular, strikes me rather as a man who would prefer to drift, expecting all to come his way with no effort on his part. That he should be required to exert himself seems not to have occurred to him.''

Emma had to agree, although she felt somewhat disloyal in doing so. "You asked earlier whether I had more reason to suspect Mrs. Stonor," she said. "Although I have no evidence, all I have learned about her confirms my suspicion. The timing, in particular, fits quite well. I wondered from the beginning what precipitated the first attack; after all, I came into my inheritance six months ago. It was an argument against either Georgiana or Charles being the would-be killer; either could have accomplished their aim far easier at home in Yorkshire. The necessity to hire a stranger almost entirely eliminated Georgiana, who is very shy. On the other hand, I was nearly run down by the coach shortly after I had observed how very intimate Mrs. Stonor and Charles were together. Also, Uncle Max has inquired into her background, which is not at all what one would guess." She told him the results of her uncle's investigation. "It seems to me very revealing of her character, not to mention her need for money!''

"Yes, indeed,'' he agreed. ''I, too, have considered her, primarily because it struck me as curious that nobody knew anything about her family or former husband, and yet she was so generally accepted. I could not make her the prime suspect, however, when I have been acquainted with you such a relatively short time, and therefore had no way of knowing what other enemies you might have garnered.'' His mouth twitched. ''I am not implying, you understand, that you have a particular talent for making enemies, merely that you have a sharp tongue, as I have before remarked, and an air of straightforward integrity that might well have clashed with someone who had a dishonest purpose.''

"I thank you for that encomium,'' Emma said dryly, ''if that is indeed what it was.'' She hesitated. ''Do you think my reasoning good? Am I right to believe it to be Lydia Stonor?''

"Yes, undoubtedly,'' he said tersely. ''But what are we to do about it?'' A reluctant smile lifted the corners of his mouth. ''I'm being foolish, aren't I? You must have a plan. You didn't take the risk of coming here just to tell me this, did you?''

"No,'' she admitted. ''I do have a plan, for which I need help, and I didn't know where else to turn.'' She drew a deep breath. Apologizing in advance for what was beginning to seem unbearable presumption on her part, she said straight out, ''Perhaps I'm asking too much.''

"You know I want to help you,'' he said in his abrupt manner, as though he had read her mind and sought to ease the way. "I offered my assistance once before."

"Yes, I know," she said, "and although it was impractical to have even considered a solution that would have so trapped us both, I believe it was your offer that gave me the courage to come to you today."

At her words his mouth compressed into a taut line as he regarded her with something very near dislike. "My willingness to lend my assistance, which I hope you don't doubt, is entirely separate from my desire to make you my wife." He paused, then continued in the same chill voice, "Although it perhaps arises from the same motivation."

Emma's heart seemed to leap out of rhythm, then resumed its steady course at a far faster tempo. What was Ware trying to say? Was he merely being polite, saying what he ought to a lady he had asked to be his wife? Or dared she read more into his words?

"Of course, I'm flattered by your confidence in my humble self," he went on, his voice now dripping with sarcasm, which he punctuated at this point by offering a mocking half-bow, "but I must ask why you chose me. Why not Linley, with whom you are also on such *intimate* terms?"

Emma held back her temper with an effort, her restraint, unusual for her, strengthened by the hope that was burgeoning in her breast. The earl, impossible though it seemed, spoke as though he were jealous.

She answered equably, "Mr. Linley would not approve of my scheme. I don't believe he thinks women should take any initiative outside the home. In any case, he is not...adventurous! Besides..." She could not resist one tiny jab. "Thanks to your unmannerly interruption, I am not presently on civil terms with Mr. Linley.''

"You don't feel you can turn to him for assistance, and yet you would become his wife?" He spoke with incredulous contempt.

Emma folded her hands in her lap and returned his gaze with a serenity she did not feel. "Why should you believe I intend to marry him? Must I marry every man with whom I dance?''

A storm was brewing in his dark blue eyes, and his nostrils flared. "Why else did you turn me down? Or have you enjoyed encouraging so many men you did not intend to have? Was it a game you played?''

Emma leaped to her feet in outrage. "How dare you? Your arrogance is unbounded! I have never encouraged *you*! Your offer came unasked—''

"And apparently unwanted,'' he returned bitterly. He lounged in a gilt-legged armchair, but his body was as tense as the string of a bow just before the arrow is sent on its deadly path. He stared up at Emma as though he hated her.

Emma could not bear it. She swung around, presenting her back to him, and bowed her head as she fought back tears.

"Emma...'' His voice was different, shaking, and she could feel, as though his warmth reached out to touch her, that he now stood close behind her. "It's unforgivable for me to reproach you, and at such a time, when you sought my help! As a gentleman...'' His large brown hands on her shoulders lightly drew her around, but then he seemed to forget what he was saying as his eyes searched her face.

Suddenly he threw back his head and gave a harsh laugh. "But I am *not* a gentleman, and so I must ask. What does forgiveness matter?" His hands tightened. "Emma, *why* did you refuse me? Your body knows you are mine! Why do you persist in denying it?"

Emma stood very still under the weight of his hands and stared up into his glittering blue eyes. Quietly she said, "I deny it only because it is not enough. How soon before your desire begins to fade? How many mistresses have you possessed and then discarded?" Her voice rose betrayingly. "I will be no man's light-skirt, tossed out on the heap."

"You would not be my mistress but, rather, my wife and, God willing, the mother of my children. How can you think I would discard you?"

She pulled from his grip but held his gaze defiantly. "I spoke only metaphorically. I have no desire to be your countess while you look elsewhere for love!"

"Emma..."

She suddenly realized she had said too much. She panicked, backing away from his outstretched hand. "Don't listen to me!" she said. "I don't know what I'm saying. I just... We are not suited."

"We are admirably suited!" he contradicted hotly.

She shook her head. "No. You have some chivalric notion now of rescuing me, and because you want me as well you are willing to offer your name. It is not reason enough for marriage."

He was staring incredulously at her. "Do you honestly believe I would saddle myself with a wife I didn't want merely to protect her? For God's sake, Emma, there are many women in this world that need help, and I have yet to ask one of them to marry me! I mentioned it to you that day merely to point out that marriage would end your problems.'' He hesitated, then a reluctant honesty compelled him to concede, ''Perhaps I *did* intend it as an inducement. I was far from certain that you even liked me, and was marshaling my arguments. Still, I can't believe you thought it my only motive!''

''I believed you also wanted me,'' Emma said truthfully. ''But wanting and love are far different emotions.''

''Oh, I want you,'' he murmured, with a caressing look that sent that familiar sweet warmth spreading through her limbs. ''But the desire I have for you won't be slaked in an hour, or a week, or a year. And I want more than to possess your body. I want...'' He suddenly broke off, then resumed, abruptly sounding weary. ''But you don't care about that, do you? What you are trying to tell me is that despite the way your body responds, you do not love me.''

As though he could no longer bear to look at her, he spun sharply away and stared out the window again. Emma could see the rigid way he held himself, the tension in his neck and shoulders, as though his body were braced for a blow.

''Well?'' he said at last, sounding impatient, as if he wished to be done with her. ''Tell me the truth, Emma!''

Emma's voice emerged as a squeak. ''Will you please tell me,'' she asked, ''why you *did* offer for me?''

He gave a brief glance over his shoulder, his expression remote and almost irritated. "Because I love you, of course," he said matter-of-factly. "You know that."

There was a long, quivering silence, in which Emma's heart hammered so hard it nearly deafened her and Ware stood so still he might have been transformed to stone. Then he turned slowly back to face her and, choosing his words with painful care, said, "You *do* know, don't you?"

"Why didn't you tell me?" she whispered.

"Because I was afraid," he said simply. "Like a coward, I hoped you might expose yourself first. Expressing emotion is not easy for me. It has been a very long time since I have done so."

What she saw on his face made Emma's heart lurch, and she was near to laughing and crying at the same time. The carefully constructed mask was gone, and the love, the tenderness, the sheer desperation in his eyes were all and more she had ever dreamed of. He had laid himself bare for her, handed her the only weapon that could hurt him, and she was humbled. She looked at his harsh, proud face and felt awe that she alone could bring him joy and passion.

"Why are you crying?" he asked in a husky voice as he tentatively touched her damp cheek with one gentle finger.

"Because I love you."

"Oh, God." He closed his eyes for an instant, then opened them to stare fiercely down at her. "Emma, are you sure? You're not taking pity...?"

"Now it is you who are being absurd!" she said tartly, blinking back her tears. "I have loved you since the first time we met and you were so very rude! I refused your offer because I could not bear to be so close to you when you did not care for me. So, you see, I was a coward also." Filled with audacity, she slipped her arms about his neck. "And I lied to you," she whispered. "Mr. Linley's kiss was *not* the same!"

A choked laugh was her answer as he pulled her into a close embrace and buried his face in the soft cloud of hair that was already sliding loose from its constraints. She felt his impatient hand plucking the pins away, and in an instant her hair tumbled free over her shoulders and back.

Ware held her a little away from him, although his hands gripped her very tightly, as though he feared to lose her. He said huskily, "I have long had an ambition to see your hair loose." A glimmer of a smile showed. "I would prefer to have it flowing about your unclothed body, as nature intended, but I am gentleman enough to defer that until our wedding night. But this I will not defer!"

And with that, his lips closed hungrily on hers, which parted instantly under his onslaught. She felt again the exquisite pressure of his long, hard body against her softer curves, the overlapping ripples of sweet sensation conjured up by his big hands, moving so freely over her back and hips and the tender skin of her neck. And how different it was to have no doubts, to know that not only desire moved him, but love as well, and that there would be a tomorrow.

When his mouth left hers, it was only to brush across her cheek, nibble gently on her earlobe, then trail tiny burning kisses down the slender column of her throat. When he encountered the coarse brown material that formed the high neckline of her gown, he muttered, in a passion-thickened but still-laughing voice, "My love, your taste in clothing is usually perfection, but this . . ."

She chuckled as she ran a loving hand along the strong line of his jaw, feeling the rough texture of his close-shaven skin. " . . . is a very *practical* gown," she murmured.

"I would like to rip it off you!" he said with sudden violence. His hands caressed her through the coarse fabric, outrageously tracing the outline of her breasts, cupping them in his palms. His voice changed, mesmerizing her, as he said, "Then I would lay you on the sofa, silken skin against velvet, and I would learn your body, from the sunlit pools of your green eyes to the sensitive arches of your feet. And you would discover that the joy of passion is not something that must be hidden in the dark, a shame to be covered when the sun shines, but one of life's greatest gifts."

His lips brushed like a breath of air across her eyelids, then closed on her mouth with a soft but insistent pressure while his tongue tasted the softness within, as though he savored a sweet wine. And when he lifted his head again, he looked dazed, like a man who had drunk too much, or perhaps not enough.

"I could touch you all day," he murmured, "kiss you without pausing for breath, drown in the feel of you."

And then his hands stilled, as though he had been jarred by his own words. Emma scarcely noticed, so lost was she in happiness. That a man should talk to her so, touch her in such an intimate way, should have been shocking; instead, she had been pressing closer

to him, arching to the feel of his hands, losing awareness of all but the glow in the blue eyes that looked at
her from beneath heavy lids, the silky texture of his
dark hair, the strength of his back and neck under the
fine linen of his shirt, the powerful muscles of his
thighs, the hand tangled in her thick hair.

She was chilled when he drew away, and she reached
out as though to hold him. He squeezed her fingers
tightly in his, but she saw the regret on his face.

"My love," he said softly, "I wish we *did* have all
day, but I fear our time is limited. Does anyone know
you are here?"

Consciousness was creeping back into her mind, as
if sunlight were slipping through cracks in a curtain.
She shook her head slightly, trying to free it from the
lassitude that clung like an early-morning fog.

Slowly she said, "I hope I'm not missed. My aunt
and uncle would be frightened!" She blinked with a
sudden thought. "How are we to explain...?"

He grinned. "Our mysterious change of heart? I
believe I will call on you in the morning, and we will
remain closeted in your aunt's drawing room for an
appropriate interval. I'm quite certain we can manage
to occupy ourselves. Then we can emerge, flushed and
rumpled, and announce our intentions to the world.
Will that do?"

She had to laugh. "Very nicely. And if I am discovered today, I will explain that we have been privately
meeting on walks. Aunt Helen will be so delighted
with the outcome that she won't care how it comes
about!"

"Speaking of outcomes—" his steady gaze held
hers "—you *do* plan to marry me?"

"Can you doubt it?"

"No." There was no laughter in his face now. "It is too late for you. I won't let you escape now!"

When his hand urged her toward the sofa, Emma, somewhat alarmed by Ware's newly serious mien, acceded to the pressure and sat, watching as he did the same.

He continued apologetically, "I dislike raising the subject again, but there is a decision you must make. As I once pointed out so clumsily, our marriage will end all threat to you from Mrs. Stonor. Obviously, we would need to elope. We cannot afford to take the chance of delaying while I seek your father's permission. But is ending the threat enough?" the earl asked, his countenance now unreadable and his voice noncommittal. "Or do you want revenge for all she has done to you?"

Emma stared into his intent face. What did he wish her to do? Depending on her marriage to settle the matter was certainly the easiest course. Papa would understand and forgive her. Once she was wed, Emma's death would serve no purpose for Lydia Stonor, who was surely too greedy to settle for an impoverished title, which was all poor Charles could offer.

"Revenge?" Emma tasted the word. "No," she said thoughtfully, "I don't want revenge, but, at the same time, I don't think my safety is enough. Lydia Stonor is dangerous, and she must not be allowed to behave so with impunity. We know what she is capable of. What is to prevent her from trying the same tricks, perhaps more successfully, on someone else? No, if it is at all possible, I would like to prove her culpability."

The reserve she had sensed in Ware was instantly gone. He smiled wolfishly. "Good," he said, leaning forward. "Then let's lay our plans."

CHAPTER ELEVEN

THE MOMENT THE DOOR closed quietly behind the butler, leaving Emma alone in the drawing room, she hurried nervously over to peer out the small bow window. The room was an upstairs one in the front of the house, but the window was hung with such a fine-patterned, heavy lace that Emma could barely see the man who was strolling casually by the house, swinging a cane. She had an impulse to yank the lace from its rod and toss it away. Although the day was overcast, outside it was bright, but in here the light only reached grubby gray fingers through the film that cloaked the glass.

Emma heard a slight sound and spun around to face the door with a sharply drawn breath, but she was still alone. Annoyed at herself for her discomposure, she closed her eyes for an instant and willed her taut muscles to relax, but still she felt as though her ears had grown larger and were reaching out for any tiny sound that might herald her hostess's approach.

If she were a member of a general's staff, she decided, she would carefully reconnoiter her surroundings now so that she could later move with confidence. She glanced about the room, which looked much as she would have expected from seeing the exterior. The row houses on this street were well kept and appeared genteel, but many were probably occupied by well-to-do tradesmen. The address was barely respectable, and certainly not fashionable. Mrs. Stonor had no doubt spent the season murmuring apologetically about how late she had arrived in London, how impossible it was to find a decent house, how frustrating it was not to rent enough space to hold even a small musicale.

Either the owner or previous renters had endowed the room with a hodgepodge of ill-matched pieces, none of which indicated that a superior sense of taste had been at work. The Egyptian craze had apparently found favor with some earlier occupant, for Emma's gaze was immediately drawn to a cumbersome sofa that dominated the center of the room. The deep red velvet seat of the sofa was slung between two enormous gilt sphinxes. A nearby small table sat upon a pedestal shaped like an Egyptian cat, which was also gilt and had slanted eyes picked out with small, glittering bits of colored glass.

The room contained a profusion of variously shaped tables, some of which were dominated by huge claw feet, and there were several armchairs covered with a particularly virulent green-and-gold-striped damask. As the wallpaper was also striped, but in a gaudy red and gold, the effect was garishly unattractive, and as far as could be from the current fashion for uncluttered lines and cool colors. Emma decided that perhaps it was just as well that the light was diffuse; at least the reds and greens and golds were somewhat muted.

Her eye was caught by the one attractive piece of furniture in the room, a walnut library table that stood against one wall. It was in the Queen Anne style, with slender, tapering legs and a delicate scroll design inlaid around the edge of the top and on the one large drawer. Emma had walked over to the table and was running her hand across the velvety wood, admiring the workmanship that had melded the mother-of-pearl and ebony with the wood, when the door opened behind her.

She turned slowly around to see Lydia Stonor walk in. Emma momentarily had the sensation of watching a cat slip into the room, silent and watchful. Like a cat, Lydia was beautiful in a vaguely silken way. The high-waisted gown in peach gauze emphasized her slender-boned grace, setting off the long, sinuous line of her neck and the faintly slanted eyes. She must have been taken aback to hear that Emma was here, and yet she had the confidence, the arrogance even, to look directly into Emma's eyes, an inquiring half smile on her red lips.

"Miss Denton!" she said. "Such a surprise. It's delightful to meet you again." Her deep brown eyes were wary, belying the polite enthusiasm.

Emma forced an answering smile, one she hoped was diffused with cordiality. "I can only apologize for not calling sooner," she said. "Charles speaks so often of you."

"How kind of you to say so."

It was as though they participated in a stage play, and neither was a good actress; the polite phrases emerged as stilted, grotesque parodies. Although perhaps that was in her imagination, Emma thought. Lydia might well think this a genuine morning call.

How long, she wondered, could she keep this up? How long would she need to? All she could do was delay and hope that, when the charade ended, Ware and his helpers had managed to take the house and were in position to listen.

"I've been so sorry not to encounter you recently," she continued with false regret. "We must have different friends."

Lydia's full red lips tightened, and Emma realized her remark had been ill-chosen, a sharp dagger pricking at soft skin.

"As I've remarked before, I haven't a relative in a position to ease my entrée," the woman said stiffly. "You are so fortunate."

"Yes, indeed," Emma agreed. "My sister and I are fully sensible of our good fortune. However," she added sincerely, "you are so very lovely that I cannot believe you have not found many admirers."

The beautiful widow gave a short, harsh laugh, her mask of easy charm slipping. "Admirers, yes; suitors, no," she said bitterly. "The ton does not welcome with open arms a lady such as myself who lacks both connections and a generous portion. Beauty alone does not adequately sweeten the package." As though she felt she had said too much, she turned away, saying, with only a whisper of sourness left in her voice, "Forgive me for my frankness. I fear my illusions have been shattered."

Emma felt a pang of pity, which she quite easily suppressed. If Mrs. Stonor believed what she said, and was truly bitter, then she was a hypocrite. Whatever she thought of Charles's fine character and handsome face, he was not acceptable to her unless he could support her in the style her ambition demanded. Society had many injustices, but Lydia Stonor was not a victim on whom Emma felt inclined to waste her sympathy.

"Have you enjoyed the season?" Emma asked. "I, for one, will be more than a little relieved when it ends. I feel as though I have made the same remarks over and over, and then heard them reflected back at me as if I spoke to a mirror. In the country I think people are less hemmed in by what they believe they ought to say."

"Oh, in the country..." Lydia made an impatient gesture. "There you feel you have been witty and original, and your partner the same, merely because you go such long stretches between seeing anyone with whom to converse. No, I prefer the gaiety here in town, the chance to dance and laugh." She abruptly changed tack. "Your brother has been so helpful to me. I believe he has taken pity on a poor, lonely widow." She spoke facetiously and her eyes challenged Emma.

Emma did not care to be mocked. She gave a kindly smile and said, "I'm so glad that Charles has gone out of his way for you. But it's in his nature, you know, to take pity on those in need. I believe it touches his heart that you should have been left alone at such a young age, and he imagines what it would be like should something of the kind ever happen to him, or to Georgiana or me. He is such a sensitive soul, he cannot bear to think of death. When our mother died he fell into so deep a gloom I feared consumption would take him. Why, I'm afraid if something happened to another member of his family, he might lose touch with reality altogether!"

Lydia gave an unconvincing chuckle. "It's sweet that you still picture him as a small boy! But he is a man now, able to turn his back on tragedy, however close to him, and take up life again with a flourish. You must have more confidence in his abilities."

"Perhaps you're right." Emma wandered closer to the door, hoping to overhear some telltale sounds. Would Lydia's servants resist the earl's men, or have the chance to give an alarm? All would be ruined, then. "Do you plan to attend Mrs. Tolles-Roper's ball on Friday?" Emma asked placidly. "I believe she expects upward of five hundred people."

"Yes, indeed. She was kind enough to send me an invitation, and your dear brother has offered to be my escort. I *do* hope that won't leave you without?"

"Oh, no." Emma smiled warmly. "The dear Earl of Ware has offered his escort." She placed the slightest, malicious emphasis on "Earl."

Mrs. Stonor put a gentle hand on Emma's arm and said in a troubled voice, "Perhaps I shouldn't say anything, but my fondness for your brother compels me to take an interest in your welfare as well."

Truer words had never been spoken, Emma reflected grimly.

"I know it's flattering to have an earl—so romantic!—courting you, but I feel I must warn you that he is known to have no intention of settling down."

Suddenly a distinct crash sounded through the closed door. Something heavy might have fallen, or perhaps a door down the hall had simply been slammed hard. The conversation was momentarily suspended as both women glanced involuntarily in that direction.

Lydia said, "Excuse me, I must check..."

Emma said hastily, "Oh, don't bother on my account. I understand how careless servants can be."

"Nonetheless..." Mrs. Stonor took a step toward the door, but before she reached it a timid knock sounded. "Yes?" she said impatiently.

The door swung open, and the butler who had earlier showed Emma up appeared in the opening.

"Ma'am, I must apologize for the disturbance. I'm afraid the maid dropped a quite heavy brass vase. Naturally, I've chastised her!"

His words tumbled one over the other, and his demeanor had none of the dignity that a superior butler should maintain to his deathbed. Sweat beaded the skin of his forehead, and his eyes flicked nervously from side to side, as though afraid to rest on one person or object. His body ostentatiously blocked the doorway, so neither woman could see out into the hall.

Mrs. Stonor's voice held a icy bite as she snapped, "Don't let it happen again! And see to it that I'm not bothered now until I call! Is that understood?"

"Yes, ma'am." He ducked his head in a nervous, submissive gesture, then retreated from the room, pulling the door to behind him.

Emma felt a tingle run down her spine. So. The final act of this play could begin. She drifted yet closer to the paneled door and took up a casual pose beside one of the numerous small tables, pretending interest in a china figurine.

"You mentioned an interest in my welfare," she said in an off-hand way. "I believe you might be just the person to assist me in arriving at a decision on what to do about some difficulties I have been having." Emma paused, letting the silence stretch. "That is, if you *are* interested."

"Naturally." The reply was no more than polite.

"I've been having some very disturbing mishaps. I'm sure Charles has mentioned them." She turned to look directly at the other woman. "I've been forced to the realization that somebody actually wants me dead!"

"No!" Lydia gasped.

"Yes, I'm afraid so." Emma shook her head mournfully. "I feel it must have something to do with my fortune, wouldn't you agree?" She didn't wait for an answer. "I hope you understand that I'm confiding in you because I feel you're so *close* to being one of the family. I know how fond of you Charles is."

"Although I would be delighted to stand as your friend," Lydia interjected blandly, "I don't like to have you misunderstand my relationship with your brother and think it greater than it is. I hope I haven't led you to believe—"

Emma cut off her retreat. "Please! You needn't say anything! I fully understand the awkwardness of your position. Charles has always been slow in coming to the point." She let her tone moderate to one of slight embarrassment. "But would you rather I not spoke? Do I presume too much?"

"No, no!" Mrs. Stonor said quickly. "I'm fascinated by your story! And, of course, concerned for you."

"Of course," Emma agreed, unable to keep the dryness entirely from her voice.

Lydia continued, "But tell me, have you found the solution to your mystery?"

Emma strolled idly about the room, so that she was forced to raise her voice to be heard by the woman who stood so still by the inlaid table. "I have my suspicions as to the identity of this person," she said, "but there is no way for me to be certain. So I have decided to change my will. I believe I will make my aunt and uncle my beneficiaries. Perhaps I won't even tell my brother or sister. Their feelings might be hurt, don't you agree?"

"I feel sure they would understand. And I commend you on your course of action," Mrs. Stonor said. "However, you really shouldn't delay. After all, an accident could happen at any time."

"Yes, I had intended to act tomorrow morning. But you positively frighten me!" She simulated a shiver. "I hate to think of missing Lady Bidwell's garden fete—it was postponed because of rain, you know. Yes, I'll do it! This very afternoon!" She nodded decisively.

"Very wise! But shouldn't you be staying close to home until this matter is solved?" Mrs. Stonor's tone of warm concern was almost convincing. "I hope you've taken precautions, so that your relatives know where you've gone. It would be so easy for you to just disappear."

"In broad daylight?" Emma chuckled. "Just as an example, I'm sure any number of people saw me come in here."

Lydia smiled warmly in return. "As you say, using my street as an example, you shouldn't depend on strangers. I doubt any of my neighbors knows who you are, and I have so many callers. If someone across the street chanced to glance out the window and see you, how likely is he to remember it? Particularly if no one traced you here at all and thought to ask neighbors."

Emma frowned. "Perhaps I *should* have been more careful. But somehow all of this seems so unnecessarily dramatic!"

"Surely Charles, at least, knows you're visiting me today?"

"Oh, no!" Emma simpered. "I wanted to surprise him with what close friends we've become. In fact, I have to admit my visit here today was the result of an impulse. I sent that silly maid of mine home—I get so disgusted with her dawdling!—and walked over here. I hope I haven't been too informal?"

"Informal?" Lydia smiled slowly. "No, I think it's delightful that you chose to drop by today. You were quite right in thinking we have a great deal to talk about. I really wish we could become sisters, but—" she shook her head pityingly "—I'm afraid I have other plans."

Emma gave one last silly moue, hoping she wasn't overdoing. "Do you mean you're already betrothed to another gentleman?"

"Oh, no," Lydia said softly. "Charles will do very nicely. Such a biddable young man! I really prefer them that way. And, of course, there's the title. Naturally, I would have preferred a grander one, but . . ." A flash of dislike showed briefly on her face before she continued, "Unlike you, I haven't the means to buy one. In any event, Viscountess Denton has a pleasant ring to it, don't you think? It will certainly open the door to many homes presently closed to me. And I understand that estate in Sussex that Charles will be inheriting is both elegant and comfortable, as well as being so convenient to London."

"That sounds remarkably like a threat," Emma said calmly. Inwardly she exulted. Lydia Stonor had slipped her neck within the snare, and it was being pulled snug with her unwitting cooperation.

"A threat? Oh, no, just a prediction. It's good to have a picture in mind of what one hopes to achieve, don't you think?" She was running a caressing hand back and forth along the inlaid surface of the library table, as if she imagined she were touching something, or someone, else.

Emma walked slowly back toward her, moving closer to the door, which seemed itself to be listening to the strange dialogue.

"How," Emma asked, a trifle sarcastically, "do you plan to bring this splendid ambition about?"

"Quite easily. You will simply disappear." Triumph was implicit in the woman's easy stance and relaxed manner. She seemed to enjoy the discussion, as though she took pleasure in her imagined power.

"I'm not entirely helpless, you know," Emma remarked. "As you've doubtless guessed, I lied about nobody knowing my whereabouts. I gave my maid strict instructions. She's my insurance."

Lydia simply laughed. "And who will believe her? I will deny that you ever arrived, and express great concern. After all, you might have vanished at any time after parting from your maid. How will it be proved you ever walked in my door? I feel confident that I have more credibility than a servant. Charles would be outraged if any accusation were leveled at me."

Emma studied her curiously. "I believe you're insane! All of the previous attempts on my life have been so carefully planned that you and I both know I could never prove your guilt! Why take such a risk now? You can't be certain about what your neighbors noticed, or, for that matter, whom I told about this visit."

"You're suggesting I give up?" She laughed again. "Is that what you hoped to accomplish by this visit? But you miscalculated! I am a gambler at heart, you see. I'm prepared to accept those risks you speak of to win the reward I seek. No, I won't return to scraping and scratching just to have food on my plate and a roof over my head. I shall throw the dice: all or nothing."

She turned, almost casually, and opened the drawer of the lovely inlaid table. Her hand dipped into the open drawer and emerged holding a long-barreled dueling pistol, which she raised so that it was pointing directly at Emma.

Perhaps because she had once before looked straight into the barrel of a gun, and yet emerged unscathed, Emma felt remarkably cool. She raised her brows with slow disdain and said, "Which of your hirelings do you plan to call now? They haven't proved very adept thus far!"

"Most incompetent," Lydia agreed. "I think we can find another way of handling it, don't you?"

Emma's legs, and even her tongue, seemed suddenly to be paralyzed, as she realized that Lydia did not intend to call a servant to do the dirty work; this time she was going to make certain, trusting no one to do what she could so easily accomplish herself. Although Lydia had only one shot, Emma stood not ten feet from her, and in these close quarters it would be nearly impossible for her to miss.

Emma's plan had gone appallingly, horrifyingly awry. Ware stood just outside the door, hearing every word, but unable to see the weapon being steadied in Lydia's hand. Nothing had been said that would make him suspect that Emma was in danger; they had never dreamed that Lydia might be prepared to commit the murder herself. It was a measure of her desperation that she would shoot Emma in her own drawing room, chancing the noise and the messy, telltale blood that would surely spread on the carpets and perhaps splatter the furniture.

Emma hadn't even had the opportunity to think, to consider alternatives, when she saw Lydia smile with soft venom. "Do you know," Lydia remarked in a conversational tone, "I have come to dislike you very much." With that the gun lifted slightly and her slender finger began to tighten on the trigger.

In that shocking instant Emma was freed from her paralysis. She screamed as she flung herself sideways, toward the refuge of the enormous red velvet sofa. All seemed to be moving in slow motion, as she was aware of the door crashing open, Lydia's eyes flicking that way, then returning to Emma as she once again took careful aim and pulled the trigger. The sound was as though Zeus, in a burst of immortal rage, had loosed his thunder in the small room. Then Emma was rolling behind the bulk of the sofa and had lost sight of Lydia Stonor's demonic form.

Emma lay gasping for breath, face nearly touching the shining gilt of the sphinx, which seemed, in her befuddlement, to be standing guard over her. Had she been shot? The other time she had felt no pain, either. Before she could recover herself to make certain, the earl had rounded the sofa and dropped to his knees beside her, urgently gathering her to him.

"Emma!" he cried, in a tone that ached with desperation, fear that he had been too late. "Are you hurt? Did she hit you? Emma, dear God, answer me!"

She was on her knees now, looking into the open terror that darkened Ware's blue eyes and reassured her, finally and forever, what she meant to this man. With a sob she threw her arms about his neck and pressed herself against his strong body. His arms closed about her in a painful grip that yet comforted as nothing else could have done.

Other men had swarmed into the room on the earl's heels and were struggling with Lydia Stonor, who seemed, in the ultimate moment of failure, to have gone completely mad. She thrashed about with amazing strength, but wildly, as if unaware of the men trying to contain her. Her head was flung back, so that cords in her neck stood out, and she was screaming, a high-pitched, inhuman wail.

Emma hid her face against Ware's broad shoulder to shut out the sight, but nothing could shield her from the sound. The screams continued to rip at her ears as Lydia was dragged into the hall and down the stairs.

When at length Ware held Emma a little away and said again, "Emma, are you hurt?" she was able to answer with frail composure and not a little surprise, "No." She gave a shaky smile. "She missed, I think because you came so fast. She knew she had lost her gamble, and she pulled the trigger only from hate, not caring that she would be heard. She couldn't bear to think of me still possessing what she wanted so badly.''

His hands on her shoulders tightened. "She is an evil woman," he said quietly.

"What...what will be done with her?" Emma asked with a quiver in her voice. The echoes of the manic screams still sounded in her ears.

"You needn't concern yourself," he answered almost roughly. "She's gone now. You'll never see her again."

"I don't want..."

He understood what troubled her before she could put it in words. "If she recovers her reason enough to stand trial, I will ask that she be exiled to one of the colonies," he said. "You will not have her death on your conscience." He stood then, with one lithe motion, and pulled Emma to her feet as well. "Her servants will need to be released, as we can't know which of them knew of her scheme and which are innocent. None resisted us, and all seem to have feared her."

Emma glanced apprehensively toward the door, which stood ajar. All was silent again.

"Can we go?" she asked.

He shook his head. "Let's wait until we're certain they're gone. There's nothing to fear here, Emma. Look around. This is just a rented house, which will forget Lydia Stonor as quickly as it has forgotten its other tenants."

He was right. The drawer to the beautiful library table was closed; not even an echo of the gunshot or her screams remained; even Lydia's scent had faded. The room had never been possessed by Lydia Stonor, and no taste of evil lingered.

"It truly is over," Emma said slowly. "I am safe now."

"Yes." His eyes searched hers. "Our trap succeeded, although I find I get no pleasure from it." His mouth twisted. "It took all my self-control to stand outside that door, my hand on the knob, and listen to her threaten you without entering! I wanted to strangle her, and I was afraid."

Emma looked at him with surprise. "Did you guess she might try to kill me herself?"

"No!" he said vehemently. "How can you think it? I would never have allowed you to step into this house if I had imagined she was willing to go to such lengths! All I knew was that she wanted you dead, and you were alone with her, a closed door between us. And when you screamed . . ."

Emma touched his cheek in comfort. "It's all over," she said. "For us. But poor Charles!"

"He's much better off," Ware said firmly, "and he will know it. Lydia Stonor never cared for him at all; she only wanted his title and the inheritance he would receive from you. What would life with her have been like? Once accepted into the ton, mightn't she have begun to imagine what prizes could be captured by a wealthy widow? How she would have loved being a duchess, for example! It makes one wonder how her first husband died! Your brother is not such a fool that he will not be able to accept that he was only besotted with her beauty; whomever he dreamed he loved did not exist."

"Perhaps," Emma agreed. "Still, I think he cared for her very much. This will be a dreadful shock."

There was a long, oddly peaceful silence, during which Emma glanced about the room, remembered the last hour, and prepared to turn her back on it. Suddenly she gave a tiny, mischievous smile and turned back to Ware.

"It's a pity..." she said thoughtfully.

"What is a pity?" he asked, rising to her bait.

She smiled up at him with all the love in her heart. "Now we have no excuse to elope. You will have to ask Papa's permission, and it may be many weeks before I will become your wife. I must confess I am unbecomingly anxious!"

"And so at last you admit it!" he said outrageously. "I have known how anxious you were for my touch since the first time we met!" Before she could protest, he bent his head so that his lips hovered only inches from hers. "But you are not as anxious as I am," he murmured. "Perhaps we *should* elope, after all." His mouth met hers with fierce need.

Explore love with Harlequin in the Middle Ages, the Renaissance, in the Regency, the Victorian and other eras.

Relive within these books the endless ages of romance, set against authentic historical backgrounds. Two new historical love stories published each month.

HIST-A-1

ATTRACTIVE, SPACE SAVING BOOK RACK

Display your most prized novels on this handsome and sturdy book rack. The hand-rubbed walnut finish will blend into your library decor with quiet elegance, providing a practical organizer for your favorite hard-or soft-covered books.

Only $9.95

Approximately 16" x 8" when assembled

Assembles in seconds!

To order, rush your name, address and zip code, along with a check or money order for $10.70 ($9.95 plus 75¢ postage and handling) (New York residents add appropriate sales tax), payable to *Harlequin Reader Service* to:

In the U.S.

Harlequin Reader Service
Book Rack Offer
901 Fuhrmann Blvd.
P.O. Box 1325
Buffalo, NY 14269-1325

Offer not available in Canada.

BKR-1

Take
4 novels
and a
surprise gift
FREE

She had the pride of Nantucket in her spirit and the passion for one man in her blood.

Until I Return

Laura Simon

Author Laura Simon weaves an emotional love story into the drama of life during the great whaling era of the 1800s. Danger, adventure, defeat and triumph—UNTIL I RETURN has it all!

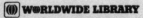

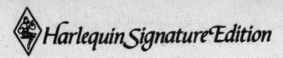

Harlequin Signature Edition

Violet Winspear

THE HONEYMOON

Blackmailed into marriage, a reluctant bride
discovers intoxicating passion and heartbreaking
doubt.

Is it Jorja or her resemblance to her sister that
stirs Renzo Talmonte's desire?

A turbulent love story unfolds in the glorious
tradition of Violet Winspear, *la grande dame* of
romance fiction.